DISTRACTIONS 3312

DISTRACTIONS 3312

VOLUME I

ELLEN SALTER CLEARY

iUniverse®

DISTRACTIONS 3312
VOLUME I

iUniverse books may be ordered through booksellers or by contacting:

iUniverse
1663 Liberty Drive
Bloomington, IN 47403
www.iuniverse.com
844-349-9409

Illustrations and photos by Ellen Salter Cleary

ISBN: 978-1-6632-0811-8 (sc)
ISBN: 978-1-6632-0812-5 (e)

Library of Congress Control Number: 2020916391

Print information available on the last page.

iUniverse rev. date: 09/23/2020

DEDICATION

Thank you to my special muses, Xedeousrel 4, for without you this book could not be done… and Ceipael 12, for helping me find the missing works I almost lost forever…

Thank you to those that believed in me, helped me with this book, and especially those who helped me start believing in myself…

CONTENTS

ACKNOWLEDGMENTS

There are many quotes acknowledging the people that said them, songs acknowledging the artists, and movies acknowledging the actors and others… There are also many that gave me the inspiration to "write a book"…so I did… actually a few. And I acknowledge these people in many ways…

Please understand…

The way this book is written is how the narrator talks and thinks as well as with the other characters. It is designed in a way to put you in the narrators perspective and understand what she is going through and why things happen the way they do. Many characters speak differently than others so the punctuation and grammar changes throughout the book.

There is a lot of confusion and a lot of inconsistencies throughout this "Distraction 3312" series… these are here to show the reader what these "entities" put the narrator and other characters through… the entities – whether Angel, Demon, or Spirit – were telling their stories as well… it is how they communicated the messages "they" wanted to tell…

All characters will be introduced to you in the same way they were introduced to the narrator… mysteriously and over the years. There are many entities that influence us and talk through us; we just don't know they are there or what their intentions are… but they are “energy without form”… whether negative or positive is how you react to a situation. You have to trust the images in your head for their descriptions. They are what you perceive them as.

Not all angels are “angels”… and not all demons are “demons”…
You just have to “pay attention”…

PROLOGUE

Plecko the woodpecker

Today is June 3, 2018
Sunday

I don't feel like adulting today. I don't feel like peopling today either. I don't feel like getting dressed. Today is what I call a "recharge day". Welcome to my world.

I am an Aries, born March 31st 1961 in the heart of the Garden State. A Jersey girl. Very proud of that fact. I was born on Good Friday at 7:25 AM in Plainfield, NJ and almost killed my mother in the process.

My father had to take care of me the first few months of my life which made an unbreakable bond that even his death almost 14 years ago has not broken to this day. I am the youngest of six children and when I was born the doctor told my mother she should have stopped at two.

Maybe I will be a squirrel today. They are so much fun to watch. Have you ever just sat and watched them play or search for the nuts you gave them in the morning? I do that every day. Squirrels and birds. They each have a personality of their own.

Piry is a very important blue jay. He is the boss. He always lets out the call to the others and takes three walnuts at a time in his beak to his nest and comes back for three more. Always three walnuts at a time and two call outs. He always says "thank you" before flying off. Pery only takes one at a time and Pury comes later when the squirrels aren't around and takes two walnuts. She doesn't like competing with them. They are too wackadoo for her.

And then there is my woodpecker friend, Plecko. I also have a cardinal friend, Polmy, that comes around once in a while and there is a dove, some robins, a few starlings and finches too. I throw out some walnuts and they share them and keep me company while I have my coffee on the patio.

I am so grateful God gave me today off. I don't think I could take another day. They say God won't give you more than you can handle, but He will push you to your limits end. I always said I wish sometimes He didn't have so much faith in me. He knows me well. He knows I have reached my limit and He did let me rest today. God is awesome.

Don't ever lose faith no matter what you go through. I would not have gotten through any of this without Him. With what I have been through many would have broken long before or just given up. I was not given a choice. I stuck it out and played the hand I was dealt because that is what we do. Deal with it. So I did. God made me a warrior. But even warriors have a breaking point. I had almost reached mine. Or did I? You be the judge.

Here is my story…

CHAPTER 1

WHERE TO BEGIN...

Goodbye to the life we knew...
L-R Ryan, Ellen, Kalan, Bandjo, Rob's Uncle John, & Jacob

Everything I do basically, is for two of my boys, Jacob, and Ryan, and my dog, Cocoa. My other two sons, Bandjo (Robert Jr.) and Kalan, have moved on long before their father died and are doing ok enough on their own. As for me; my purpose in life seems to revolve around the two that stayed with me to the end and I am trying to get them ready for when I am no longer.

No one is here forever and I am no exception. I have to get them ready for my mortality. They had to stick it out with me and put up with the Hell their father put us through so my purpose is to see to it they get what they need to get through this life… no matter what.

I see to it they pay their part of the rent when the disability allotment comes in. That comes first without fail. Insurances must be paid as well. Then utilities, then the rest get paid with what is left. I make sure we have food for the month (which we barely make it but somehow always do), and I make sure Jacob got to work on time and kept in contact with his employers. I advocate for them, and I take them to appointments and set up their next, take them shopping, get them medications... as I can (Medicare does not cover everything and it gets quite expensive).

Some medicine I had to fight for and find special doctors for. I do most of the food storage, preparations, cooking, cleaning and since I am the only driver I do all of the driving. If there is any car care needed, I have to get it done. They help pay car insurance and help pay for gas when I need them to. We share all of the household expenses. This is our apartment not just mine. All I ask for is a little help keeping the place clean.

They are responsible for the bathroom between their rooms, their bedrooms, their laundry, and dishes. Maybe straighten up the living room area once in a while by the games. Not much. I take care of everything else plus my own area. When they don't do their jobs in the kitchen, I can't do my job. It holds up production and I start getting upset. And when Mom's not happy, they know it. Well it was working fine until... stuff happened.

What stuff? Well there are a few things I will call "distractions", or "squirrel syndrome". Most people when they have things to do they get their lists in order or "ducks in a row" and they get things done. Me? Oh no. I do not have ducks and they are not in a row...

I have squirrels… and not only are they at a party but they are at a "rave". For those who don't know what a "rave" is – it is a wild party held illegally hidden from the real world to put it mildly. Mostly for real party animals and my squirrels love to party.

So I am constantly distracted sometimes for hours without even realizing it. Not intentionally mind you, it just happens no matter how hard I try to stay focused on the task at hand.

One day, Archangel "Sir Chamuel" (he sounds like a southern gentleman) actually showed me just how much of a distraction these "squirrels" can be.

Let me explain…

I have a pendulum I use with an application on my phone called "Color Note". It keeps notes and sometimes gives you options of words or phrases commonly used. If you don't find the word you are looking for, you have to type it in. Some of "them" were lazy and kept circling words to get the one word they wanted to come up instead of just typing what they wanted to say.

Others got right to the point and left when they got finished with what they had to say. When this happened something else would take over the conversation and I didn't always know when it would happen until the note started to "not make sense". And, when they caught on to this, some of them would announce they were done or simply say good bye or good night. But they didn't at first for months, which is why I got so confused and distracted. My OCD (Obsessive Compulsive Disorder) would kick in and I would have to try to figure out the messages, which would take hours without me realizing it.

This is a message "Archangel Chamuel" was giving me in that app that I have on my phone using an amulet for a pendulum to circle the words he wants to use. I thought it was only a couple of minutes. But he showed me the time stamps we started then the current time…

We started at 2:38 AM but it was well after 4 AM by the time we finished.

Archangel Chamuel
Sat, Sep 22, 2018, 2:38 AM

I am not going back home again with you please call your parents again tomorrow morning to see what you're going to deliver for me to do that again because they want people that don't care who can make it to the hospital where you were born and have them come from that way there and I think we should go back and take them away to see the faces of my children who would never have been looking and would say they were just talking crazy stuff about me when there had zero tolerance over time they didn't get through them with my family or something neurology in order you were able to keep moving things together before and it would make sense that you're doing what is the text to make this happen again I just think about what happened last weekend when you were trying to guess which would take him away so he must not use this method and if he's the last man who would think he's gonna become more serious he can be an atheist because the least people would know about this situation that I can understand the problem with this crap is because his mother was very poor to him when you see her now I'm going out there will help them with their own lives for you.

And if he doesn't seem more honest than the message he should make the wrong choice but it has.

This happens every night with some good ones for everyone except me and you can have it all.

I will get some help from you when he says that you were talking like you know where the money my zakaria would come to get him in there too many friends but they can't afford anything but he's gonna do something wrong then I probably should just get them moving from that point into our system for one hour at some other hour before they can be done before you start looking to go back up into my pocket in an empty chair at your door with some help with you running around for about five to seven hours for an amount that could help keep them safe as much after your parents have completed an entire school trip you are having trouble staying awake before and when you're done getting out on this show you just haven't noticed how long this episode was going on right now but it's going well in that time frame that would come with me.

I just have enough time that you're trying not to get cold enough and do something about that one day from here to a place to sleep for your dad is in bed with your boyfriend you want it there to find something like him but he's never really bothered anyone with that little idea where it comes out of that kind anymore because he doesn't really care who he has as long as he has someone.

You need someone who wants you for being you and not trying to make you something that you are not.

But you know you have to get away from him in order to find another person.

And you look like you have to get to sleep.

See you soon

This is what the entities would do to distract me only I didn't realize it until he pointed it out to me when he wrote that note. This has been going on for the past couple months now, *since I got the pendulum*, and I did not know it was happening. And this is after they learned how to use it. Before it was much worse. I still have to decipher the messages but some are better than others and yet again… some are near impossible.

I also didn't add my part of the conversations… which made it even harder to figure out… some messages were responses to thoughts I had as well…

After I read it a few times, I called both of my Moms... Momma, Eleanor and Mom in law, Rita. He did say to call my "parents". Plural. So I did. Found out after talking to both of them he was talking about someone else that I didn't expect. It took a very long time to figure out what he was talking about but once I did, it all made sense.

Some of the things he said were metaphors and some were referring to people or entities' names. He referred to them by what they said or did and used that as their name. That is in a lot of the messages I got from "them". It took me a long time to figure that out. I just thought it was a code or something…

For example, "*I am not going home*" is actually the name he used for a certain entity he was talking about... "*people that don't care who can make it*" was another entity, "*the hospital where you were born*" was a certain place but not directed at me but someone else and it was not the one I was born at. "*have them come from that way there*" which is where the person he was talking about is from, and so on. So much to decipher… not to mention the grammar and punctuation… or lack thereof.

But he was telling me the first two entities he was talking about wanted me to look insane and the actual people he was referring to really thought I was. The personalities also came out much later so I had no idea what was going on until I deciphered a few other messages. Then this started making sense.

Like for another instance in the last paragraph he said *"your dad is in bed with your boyfriend"* … what he was telling me was my boyfriend was being used as a "vessel" by the entity "they" referred to as "The Father" specifically… very unsettling… kinda freaked me out a bit… *one of the main reasons I am now "single" and not looking to go into any kind of relationships at the moment.*

That is just one of the many distractions or "squirrels" I deal with all the time. There are so many things that kept me from doing what I needed to do. Important things didn't get done until it was too late or bills were getting overdue or past due or somehow I would be late for this or that and missing important events and couldn't understand how this could be?

And who is this "*Zakaria*" he mentioned? I found out much later, he is his "muse" or "child that assists him and helps find things".

"I don't know when it started but it has been happening for quite some time."

CHAPTER 2

OUR NEW LIFE...

The magnolia trees arching saying "welcome to your new home"...

What brought us here to Lawrenceville? I have no idea. We were looking for a two bedroom apartment with a den because that is all we could really afford at the time. Even that was going to be rough.

It was shortly after my husband passed away and we were losing the house and really had nowhere else to go. We had looked at a few places but they had income requirements. Being on disability meant a fixed income. My husband was gone. The disability was all we had to work with.

It was me with a degenerative bone disorder topped out at 252 pounds, two adult autistic sons; one of which has a seizure disorder and the other one is an introvert that can't handle noise, or people, for that matter. Both overweight and have psychotic issues, and an 11 year old therapy dog, I trained myself. I was 54 at the time.

We were getting discouraged when we got a phone call from Avalon Apartments in Lawrenceville, NJ… Mercer County, just south of Princeton.

We didn't call them, they called us. My name was out there and I had been looking and not finding… they found us. I didn't think to call so far south.

We were looking in Middlesex and Somerset counties staying in the areas where we were familiar. I knew the towns I was searching in and we knew people there and they knew us. We also knew where everything was and all our friends were there. It was our comfort zone.

I thought it was strange for a complex to call us but our name was out there and the girl did say she found us on "apartments.com" or something like that. Only thing was it is in Lawrenceville, past Princeton, about 12 minutes from the Pennsylvania border, and about an hour away from where everything is that we were familiar with in Bound Brook. But we came to check it out anyway.

My cousin, Cyndi, and my sister, Sandy, came with me to check it out as well. They had been helping when they could and were happy to check it out with me.

This particular apartment complex didn't do an income requirement, only a credit check. Ryan's was perfect. He was working on it with his credit card through the bank last year with the money he got from when he was hit by a car while he was walking Cocoa. My credit was shot because of the house and Jake didn't have any credit because of the doctor bills.

The house taxes and bills used up a lot of the money Ryan got and Rob bought a computer he never got to use. It just sat in the box for a few months … we weren't allowed to touch it. Ryan didn't get to do what he wanted with the money, but at least he got the "starter" credit card… which built up his credit.

Ryan saved us. So with his credit, and some of the money we had left from the funeral expenses, we got the apartment. Because Cocoa was a therapy dog, they waived the $500.00 pet fee plus the extra $150.00 a month "pet rent". And it was one of the few places that allowed pets.

Now being where we are is exactly where we needed to be. I just didn't know it at the time. But we were about to find out.

It was February 5, 2016 when I answered Ayanna's email to look at the apartment, and we were moved into the handicap apartment, 3312, by February 17, twelve days later.

It was like a Godsend.

We were meant to be here. Everything we need is right here. Princeton University, Princeton hospital in Plainsboro, where Jake's new neurologist practices, Philadelphia Hospital for Neuroscience where my husband went for his seizures, is only forty-five minutes away and I-95 is a block away off of US Route 1... which is easily accessible right down the street.

And a bonus! Right smack dap in the middle between Six Flags Great Adventure to the east and Sesame Place to the west! AWESOMENESS!!!

Shopping and dining is everywhere, with Quakerbridge Mall literally right next door, K.C. Prime Restaurant right up the street (Bandjo took us once before – amazing yums!), Motor Vehicles down the street, Mercer Mall with Shop-Rite, Petco, Joe Canal's Discount Liquors, and a lot of restaurants on the other side of US Route 1 and across from that, is Nassau Park Mall with Target, Michael's, Wegmans, Home Depot, Dollar Tree, Best Buy, Walmart and PetSmart. Sam's Club was there until Costco was finished in the parking lot between Avalon Apartments and eaves of Avalon. Everything is minutes away or within walking distance, but yet I am not on the highway.

Everything we need is right there where we need it - but yet, it is countryside.

We have the south side handicap apartment on the first floor facing the woods. (The sunny side.) It is a three bedroom with two full bathrooms... I have my own bathroom in my own area of the apartment along with a kitchen/laundry room, dining room large living room... and outside the living room we have a patio with two beautiful magnolia trees arching together as if to say "Here you are! This is your new home! Welcome!"

And then there is the forest across the parking lot. The animals there come to visit from time to time. We have everything we need here and if something breaks maintenance comes and fixes it. All I need to do is call and it is done. So much stress relief. I bake the guys' cookies and brownies as a thank you and I am always on the top of the list and the first one who gets the job ticket gets to fix the apartment. They do love my cookies and brownies.

That first night was the first time I felt like I was home since I was a child. We picked our rooms, set up the air mattresses and made them up, started unpacking stuff, and got ready to make dinner. We will make a trip to that house tomorrow. But at least we would never have to sleep in that nightmare of a house again.

Sandy and Cyndi came to help set up the apartment and get us settled in and my sister even took Cocoa for a walk to explore and found a few of the "puppy" stations while I went and got some groceries to start us up with, and Cyndi put the antique silver aluminum tray as a back splash for the stove which gave a unique touch.

We got the apartment looking nice in no time... except the only furniture we had was the oak dining room table and chairs with a the griffin patterns carved in the chair backs that my mother gave us, and the nice package of throwaway dinnerware Rob's sister, Gina gave us.

We also had air mattresses from the camping trips the boys and their father went on with the boy scouts. And we used the seats from the minivan to use in the living room to sit on, a couple fold up banquet tables to put the two TVs on, and a set of four little wooden TV trays to use as nightstands or end tables.

We were able to grab some plastic storage bins of stuff and my cedar hope chest my father made for me when I got married. *There was no way I would leave that behind.* I also took my father's rocking chair I got when he passed away. I keep that in my room and it is my favorite place to sit. It is like he is there and I can almost feel his hugs when I curl up in it with the afghans my mother crocheted for me.

We left the rest of the furniture we had at the house. It was mostly destroyed and heavy and I had no way to bring it if I wanted to.

We left a lot of things behind. The bed Rob spent the last years of his life in was not coming with me. *There was no way I was taking that. (I have my reasons.)* The boys' beds also needed replacing. They were pretty much shot as well. We took what we could. The rest we had no choice but to leave behind.

We had very little help to get a lot of the stuff and even if I had the help... where would we put it? *A full sized colonial house was twice the size of the new apartment plus it had an attic and a basement... four levels in all moving to one level... plus all we acquired the 24 years we were stuck living there.*

The storage unit we were renting was already getting full and I didn't even know what was going in it because I was busy with taking care of Rob until he died, and with Jake and the seizures he was having and his doctor appointments, his surgeries for his back, not to mention trying to figure out how to get Rob's ashes to Kansas to be buried with his birth father, Harvey, on top of trying to sell the house and find a new home for Jake, Ryan, Cocoa and myself.

We grabbed the important things and left as fast as we could.

The day before we were supposed to move, Jake had a grand mal seizure. The last nightmare of that "Labyrinth of the Minotaur's catacombs" as Jake would call it. I could never understand why he called it that but it is what he referred to it as. I went with Jacob to the emergency room while Ryan packed stuff to take to the apartment as his friend, Josh, helped him and kept him focused.

Everything and everyone was referred to as a mythological being or place to Jake. Some will be revealed as the stories go on. Two of his father's personalities were "Oranos (Father of the Titans and the oppressor that possessed Prometheus) or Prometheus (the liver thing)... according to what mood Rob was in. But Jake referred to me as "Rhea" - the mother of the gods. Why he refers to me as Rhea I don't know - but he does. He even got me a stone he calls the "O*mphalos Stone"* that he had gotten from a Fur-Con he went to.

If you know your Greek mythology, Rhea was the wife of Cronus. Cronus was the Titan that devoured his children when they were born for fear of them overpowering him as he overpowered his father... Oranos. Since they are immortal they didn't die as Cronus swallowed them whole.

When Zeus was born instead of giving him to Cronus, Rhea gave him a rock and put Zeus on an island to hide him from his father and when Zeus grew up he rescued his brothers and sisters from his father Cronus and defeated him and became head of Olympus.

Jake still has the stone plus a couple more. Ryan has a collection of stones too. And I have quite a few in a collection of my own. Each stone has its own story. Every single one... however some of them like to change...

...every four days. Wednesdays and Saturdays.

CHAPTER 3

CLOUDS COMING

Zupiter's clouds

Today Jake has an appointment with the neurologist. I absolutely adore her. She has practically saved his life. She still swears by the pharmaceutical anti-seizure medications but at least she listens. It looks like we found the correct combination of medication for him to be on but a lot of damage has been done because of the wrong medications that were not working.

With the wrong medication, I had to practically walk on eggshells… He had gotten to a point where just the sound of my voice would set him off.

He is my first born. 10 pounds 2 ½ ounces, 22 ½ inches long. Due May 20, 1985 (which was my Dad's birthday) born June 11, 1985 at 12:22 AM. Just after midnight… 3 weeks late. He was finally induced on June 10, 1985. I was in hard labor for 16 hours straight.

It was supposed to peak, and then go down, then a few minutes later peak, then go back down. I peaked and stayed there for the entire 16 hours. The doctor never did an ultrasound, or anything. I had toxemia from the third week of my pregnancy. He should've taken him early but instead he let me go three weeks late.

Now, mind you, my pre-pregnant weight was barely 100 pounds soaking wet and I am small boned and 5' 2 3/4". I delivered at 180 pounds and lost 20 during delivery. Jacob was 10 pounds of that.

Rob said he had to grab the doctor by the throat to convince him to take the baby out after I begged him to "please take the baby; I just can't do this anymore".

They hadn't been checking on my progress very much or if they were I didn't see them. I was alone most of the time in a labor room that had seven other unoccupied beds. But Rob would be in and out. Back then, he was pretty good with me. He would still come home drunk but at least I got attention at the time. We lived at my mom and dad's house the first five years we were married; until Jacob was around four.

After they finally came in and checked me, and I was still only at one centimeter, they decided to do an emergency C-section. Since Rob was a registered mid-wife, he was allowed in the delivery room. All I remember was crying out and a mask going over my face, my arms outstretched, legs straight, next thing I knew they put Jacob next to me to kiss my baby and told me I have a son.

I could not move but they wanted me to hold him and I couldn't. I was so afraid of dropping him. I asked them to please take him so I don't drop him. I was still so out of it from the anesthesia.

In recovery, the doctor came in and I said to him: "I don't know how he fit."

He said: "He didn't, that's why we had to take him. If we let him continue he would have been crushed and you would have been split open. We had to cut you twice because the normal size incision wasn't large enough for his head. You both would have died."

According to my Mom when he was born the nurse said, "She had the baby. Do you want to know what the baby is?"

My mother said "We will wait for the father to come out and tell us.

Then the nurse said, "Well, there are girl babies and there are boy babies and there are bruisers and let me tell ya boy is he a bruiser!"

…so much for waiting for the father to tell them the sex of the baby.

When Rob finally went to talk to the family, he told them the statistics and all they could think about was; "is there anything left of Ellen? Wow 10 pounds?" He was huge!

Now at my baby shower the baby clothes I got were for a newborn... up to 7-8 pounds. Jacob was 10 pounds 2 ½ ounces at birth; he didn't fit in any of it. When he got home ten days later he weighed a whopping twelve pounds. Rob had to get a whole new wardrobe for him before we were released from the hospital.

He was jaundice and I needed to stay for the C-Section to heal and to also clean out the toxemia. Back then doctors were in charge of our care… not insurance companies.

When it was time for the hospital baby pictures the photographer was in the nursery and Jacob was in there as well, so I don't understand how he missed him. I mean how can you miss a 10 pound baby? He was in the nursery so there was no reason for the photographer not to get his picture. But he missed Jacob.

The nurses never told me he got missed and I didn't know the procedure because he was my first born. I did ask about the pictures and they did say the photographer was there and would be in touch so I left it at that.

Rob told me the doctor used spoons to pull him out instead of using his hands and got him in the back of his neck and on his nose between his eyes and

clouds coming

Zupiter was calling me outside to see the clouds. This is what I mean about the distractions. I would be doing something and they would call me out to look at something they wanted to show me or they needed to tell me something.

I would be trying to work and I would get distracted and not be able to get back to that part until months later. This particular incident was at night when Zupiter called me to come out… but the sight was amazing.

The clouds were hard to see at first but then, with the moon light, you could see them... roses... big giant blue and white roses; at least a half dozen of them. Wow what a sight! Then he told me to take pictures of the next set of clouds, so I did. When I looked at the pictures, there were faces in the clouds. Barely visible… but they were there just the same.

Who is Zupiter? … It took me a while to find out about him too…

CHAPTER 4

MY BOO BEAR

Ryan, Christmas 2016

Jake makes the best coffee. Brings me coffee almost every morning, perfect every time. And when I thank him, he always says "of course" with a smile and is very happy.

Today it is in Ryan's "You Rock" cup he got from my oldest brother, Butch and Susan on his 21st birthday at "Cahoots" in Middlesex. He refused to touch alcohol before he was legal and for his first legal drink, he wanted a Sam Adams beer.

Of course he didn't like it – he is a vodka drinker like his mother. He prefers his vodka with tonic, or if it is Grey Goose, he likes it as a martini. He likes the "old man" drinks, but he likes the good stuff; Zyr and Crystal Head are his favorites, then Gray Goose, even Absolut but sometimes when he knows we are on a tight budget he will settle for Pinnacle… Smirnoff is strictly for cooking…not drinking.

He is quite the connoisseur when it comes to vodkas, even now at 24. I prefer flavored myself, pineapple is my favorite. Cherry is good too... but that's just me.

Ryan is also very particular about other things as well. He considers himself a wizard type. He works with magic and has a gift with finding the "itchy spot we can't reach" so he knows where to scratch and usually gets it. He does give the best hugs… when he gives them.

He is, what is known as, an "introvert". He cannot handle being around a lot of people so he hides a lot… and he hears everything. He even hears bits and pieces of the conversations from the third floor. He can also hear cars on the highway. I mean he hears everything. He wears headphones to muffle out some of the sound. In the old house, he would even hear the ants and termites in the walls. No exaggeration.

Ryan and Jake are both autistic. They focus on one thing and become experts very quickly at that particular thing they are interested in. Jake was 6 years old when he beat The Legend of Zelda in one day… that's how we found the hidden second game… he beat that in two days. (My Auntie Marlene gave us the console and a couple games to start with… Zelda and a Mario Brothers game. Bandjo and Jake would play for hours.)

Ryan could also tell you everything there is to know about the world of Zelda, Link, Hyrule and its creator. There are so many other things. Ask him what happens when you hit enter with the Google search bar empty and he will tell you all kinds of reasons why you do not want to go there. He has a very strange sense of humor, loves Monty Python, and quotes everything…verbatim.

He is very animate when he gets upset even when he is dead wrong about something there is no arguing with him. He is convinced he is right and you cannot change his mind. In his mind he is right and that is that, if you do not see it his way you are done to him. But when you ask him to do something he has no problem doing it. He is right there to help.

The other day we went to the store and there was an elderly man in a wheelchair by himself trying to get himself and his chair into his car; alone. Ryan, being an Eagle Scout, went and asked him if he could help. Of course, the man was grateful. He helped him into the car and folded up the wheel chair and put it into the car for him. It gave Ryan a sense of purpose again. Made him feel good and he smiled.

I love seeing him smile. His father beat him for smiling when he was 12 years old. It took a lot of work to make him not afraid to smile again. His father did a lot of damage to him and his brothers. Most of what was hidden from me during Boy Scout camp outs and when I was at work or I was not there to protect my boys from the monster that was growing in their father's head.

A lot of damage they kept hidden and quiet about. The monster made them keep his secret from me until it was too late.

I found out much later what happens in scouts, stays in scouts… unless Ryan is the one being bad. It didn't matter if he was defending himself or retaliating. Doesn't matter what was done to him or what drove him to the action of what he did; only what he did.

After one of the camp outs we had a picnic at the scout master's house. It turned out to be an intervention to me and Ryan. Guess everyone else knew what was going on except me. If I did I would have pulled him from scouts a long time ago.

So many times I was powerless to do anything and a lot I just plain didn't know about until much later. Rob was supposed to be taking care of Kalan and Ryan. As far as I knew they were learning how to survive in camp like how to start a proper fire, how to pitch a tent, stuff like that. I did not know about the torment the scout masters were allowing until later. They used the line: "boys will be boys".

At the time, Ryan was on Adderall, which the school system had forced me to put him on when he was 3 years old. Technically, he should not be on it until 5, and off of it before the age of 14. At this time he was 16. It does cause psychotic behavior in prolonged use and also suicidal tendencies.

I was now forced to take Ryan to a psychiatrist at a clinic. She put him on 3 more anti-psychotic drugs including Cymbalta, Risperdal, and Abilify and did not take him off of the Adderall. Within 2 months he gained 60 pounds and stretch marks all over him. He no longer smiled and was more of a zombie just going through the day, hiding. My Boo Bear was not my Boo anymore.

He was also sent to an out of district school because the regular school couldn't deal with him. *They actually sent him home one day because of flatulence…farting. Are you kidding me? They sent him home because he passed gas in class.* It isn't because he was bad, just the other kids were very mean and Rob kept insisting it was Ryan's size that was his problem and he wouldn't let anyone else speak.

Ryan was small for his age but not that small. (his brothers Jake and Kalan are both over 6 feet…Ryan is 5' 7", Rob, himself was 5' 9"). The monster in Rob's head had already started taking over and repeating things and not listening and not allowing me or anyone else to speak, including the teachers and Child Study team. No one could convince him his size was not the issue.

As a child, Ryan was happy go lucky and very impatient. I remember when he had just turned 4 years old he wanted to go trick or treating and got tired of waiting for someone to take him. He was dressed up as a pumpkin and ready to go but I was making dinner, Rob and his step father, Jim, and Rob's sister Gina, were all still working, and Bandjo (15) went with his friends. Jacob (10) and Kalan (5 ½) were patiently waiting.

Ryan got out when I had my back turned. A neighbor called and told me Ryan was there and walked into their house asking for the candy. Good thing they knew us. Jim got home by then and went to get him and just brought him home.

We had to wait for Rob to get home to take the boys out. Bandjo got home as well so him, his friends, and Rob finally took the boys trick or treating and got a ton of candy... I think that's why it is Ryan's favorite holiday... he has good memories of that. And he loves pumpkins – especially pumpkin pie... when the season comes, he looks for the pumpkin pie ice cream from "Turkey Hill"… absolutely loves it.

Ryan was due October 8, 1991 but since he was presented as breech, the clinic doctor decided he needed to take him a few days before. He was born by planned C-section on October 3, 1991 at 10:47 AM at Robert Wood Johnson Medical Center, another teaching hospital in New Brunswick, New Jersey. We decided to go to this one because it was not a

Catholic Hospital and I wanted to "close the factory" so to speak and the St. Peter's Hospital doesn't do birth control.

The clinic doctors were much more attentive with me than the private doctors I had with Jakies. I had toxemia with all three pregnancies from the first few weeks. With Ryan, I didn't confirm my pregnancy until I had already started my second trimester.

Rob said he didn't want any more and he tried to make me abort Kalan when I was pregnant with him but I wouldn't have that. It didn't take much convincing as Rob knew I couldn't and there was no reason to. I didn't want to admit I was pregnant again because Kalan was still only just under a 1 year old baby himself. He hadn't even started walking yet.

Knowing my past history with the previous pregnancies, the doctors kept a closer eye on me, not to mention I was now 30 years old. I also decided this would be my last child so we planned on getting my tubes tied as well.

Ryan kept hiding from the ultrasounds so I thought sure I was finally going to have the little girl I always wanted. So when I went in to have him, I was awake and had what was called a "saddle-block" or local anesthesia so I could see everything. *However the mirrors weren't set in the right position so I didn't see anything...*

Rob was allowed in this time as well. When the doctor took him out, Rob said, "it's another boy El".

All I could do was cry... they thought I was crying because I did not have the little girl I so much hoped for... I was crying because I was overwhelmed, my emotions just spilled over and I was relieved he was out and alright.

The doctor and Rob both asked, "are you sure about the tubal ligation".

I was in tears and crying but very serious when I told them: "I can't do this anymore. I am done. I can't go through this again."

While in the hospital, I told them I was not leaving without him and I knew with the Rh factor and, like his brothers, and since he had his father's blood type and not mine, jaundice was imminent. I told them to get him under the UV lights when I was done feeding him.

The schedule was fine until the next day they were taking a longer time than usual and all I wanted was the morphine drip out of my back and asked for Tylenol instead. The morphine wasn't doing anything because the catheter seemed to have been pushed out of the blood vessel it was in. It was going into the bandage instead of the vein. I really didn't want my baby starting his life on morphine to begin with and since I was breast feeding, I wanted that thing out as soon as possible. I have a high tolerance to most pain and Tylenol worked just fine.

When I went to get him from the nursery, there were three nurses chatting in another section waiting for newborns to come; but not watching the day old babies. They were all sleeping but when I looked at the incubator, Ryan's mask had gone askew and was not covering his eyes! Not to mention the fact he was covered in poop! I was livid!!!

I went ballistic on the nurses and they came running! They were much more attentive with him after that.

Never piss off an Aries from New Jersey especially where her children are involved. That is where "Momma Bear's" claws come out.

Ryan did not leave my sight after that. So when he had to be under the lights I stayed there with him.

Because we were now living at Jim's house, we were sleeping in the living room on a sofa bed until the basement was finished for us to move down there.

How we lost the apartment we had in August just before Ryan was born… another story…

Rob and his dad, Jim, worked on it every weekend but it took a few months to finish. So when I tried to feed Ryan, my father in law wanted to watch. (Jim adopted them when Rob was six.)

If I wanted any privacy I had to go in the bathroom and lock the door. He would stand at the bathroom door and continue his story he was telling at the time. He just creeped me out. I was so stressed from him, I couldn't breast feed and had to give up so Ryan was nursed only 3 weeks instead of the 6 months I was supposed to.

When we did move to the basement, I was bottle feeding him by that time when I noticed Ryan did not "look at me". He seemed to try but could not focus... he kept looking away. Now we already knew Jake is autistic and one of the symptoms is avoiding eye contact. So I was alarmed a bit. He was diagnosed with "infantile autism" at age 2.

We didn't know he needed glasses until he went to preschool. That's when we found out the extent of the damage to his eyes the UV lights had done. He needed a very strong prescription but Medicaid would only get the cheapest available. He needed "coke bottle" size lenses that were too heavy for his little nose to hold up so they were constantly falling off.

Mananael, "I am not here but the father was very happy about his work with his father. It should make your eyes at any higher levels as much of the time to take you seriously but it's the perfect day in my room so much easier but the guy in his own house doesn't feel safe for his past to go with their work on face time at age which will make me a friend request because it makes him an awesome guy and I am an amazing warrior who can beat the demons!!!"

Manael, "Clean"

I guess I have to go because Manael wants me to get started on cleaning… and his little sister Mananael is here to get me started in the kitchen as well.

CHAPTER 5

HURRICANE FLOYD

water receded a bit to where we could rescue the wagon and bronco

Rob coming back after assessing some of the damage on the shed after the water started receding

He was such a jerk at times… most of the time. Why did I put up with him? Vows… Love, honor, cherish for better or worse, richer or poorer, through sickness and health until death do us part may God be my help…

To me a vow is stronger than a promise. It involves a promise to God. I do not break my promises. I especially do not break my promises to God. No. You do not break a promise to the Lord. You just don't.

He wasn't always a jerk. He was a good worker and what he did was the best work a man could do. And when he was sober or even just a little "high" from smoking, he was really awesome. He was a perfectionist so he made sure the work he did was the best. He was also fast and efficient and wouldn't leave the work until it was completed.

He would work through lunch and rarely took a break. He always stood tall and straight and always used a napkin. He was very particular with his appearance as well… not to mention he played beautifully on the guitar… especially that "pinky kicker" which gave it a special twang. He had a style of his own that I just loved listening to. He was loved by just about everyone who knew him.

As far as I know Robert was not physically cheating at the time. Mentally was another story but physically, no. What was I supposed to do? He was a narcissist. You can't prove abuse with a narcissist. They are perfect. And now he was sick. If I were to leave now, what would that make me? No, I had to take it to the end. And I couldn't nor wouldn't quit on him…I loved him.

The only time he was "different" was when he drank, the problem was, he was always drunk when he came home…Yukon Jack was his drink of choice before it changed to Dewar's…Yukon he was horrible, and mean, Dewar's wasn't so bad. People didn't understand how the different alcohols made his personality change… Vodka made him verbally abusive and tequila… he became physically abusive. He mostly stayed away from white liquors. But he also stayed away from me when he was sober… Grand Marnier was another but he would only have a double shot in a snifter glass that he would "warm up" and watch the colors of the fire as it burned out in his glass… he was mellow with that.

Besides how long will it be right? I can take it. I put up with it for 20 years what's a couple more? We have money in the bank, a fixer upper house we bought from his step father, the two main cars paid off, three classic cars he paid cash for in the yard and a mortgage that isn't too bad. Taxes are a bit high but we should be ok. He will get better and get back to working and we will get back on track to where we were before.

This will all be over and he will get better and get back to the way he was before, right?

We were still in denial at the time. It was June of 2003, the day we signed the papers for the house, when Rob had his first stroke. We had $20,000 in the savings and he was making $80,000 a year plus bonuses and had a nice title to boot. With my 12,000 a year and his bonuses, together we were making over $100,000 a year so we did well.

We had a 2001 Chrysler Town & Country minivan that I had to use and after a few months he got the 2001 Mustang V6 convertible. The '66 and '68 mustangs and the '68 bronco didn't have air conditioning so he needed a car for work. Otherwise if I wanted a vehicle, I had to take him to work. I was not "allowed" to drive "his cars". *The classic cars were standard transmission and after the incident with the '62 ranchero… ah no.*

I was working at the school so I didn't have to be home with my father-in-law. We didn't know Rob had a stroke. He was in Maryland at the time and it was just after midnight. He was hungry and stopped in the hotel bar and asked for anything they could find. The bartender found some buffalo wings with bleu cheese dressing. Rob doesn't eat until the job is finished and he was supervising an installation for the company he worked for, so by the time he was done he was ravenous.

When he got to his room, he ate the wings, got a shower, then, what he described, the most excruciating pain on the one side of his head which got super-hot and he started throwing up most of the night. He went to work in the morning and threw up some more then drove the convertible up I-95 from Maryland to NJ to close on the house stopping to throw up then getting back on the road again. This was June 19, 2003… Thursday.

When we got home from the mortgage signing he went straight to bed and got up for work Friday Morning. It was my last full day working at the school but when I came home I was surprised to see the convertible in the driveway. Rob was home already. He is never home. I went to check on him and he said he just didn't feel good so I let him sleep. He slept all weekend.

I went to work on Monday and he was getting in the shower when I left. I was getting ready for 8th grade graduation when I got the call to come home. Rob got dizzy in the shower. His side went numb and when I got home he told me to call the doctor's office. They told him to get to the hospital immediately.

Doctors did a CT scan and confirmed it. Rob had a bleed in his right front temporal lobe. This would be his first of four strokes. He was 44. After spending hours in the emergency room, he was flown by helicopter from Somerset Hospital to Jefferson Hospital for Neuroscience in Philadelphia to see Dr. Rosenwasser, top in his field. My sister and I drove there to meet him.

What happened? Where did this come from? It was a ticking time bomb in his head we found out he had 4 years before… we just thought we had more time…

It was on September 16th 1999 Bound Brook, NJ… Hurricane Floyd came through… on our 16th anniversary.

We were supposed to go out for dinner that night. It was the only time I got attention; our anniversary, Valentine's Day and his birthday and maybe my birthday. I wasn't his mother so for Mother's day - I got nothing. We usually went to his mother's because it was close to her birthday. But Father's day… we made a big fuss over him.

Christmas was for his family. Thanksgiving was my Mom and Dad because it was close to their anniversary, and Easter?...was a tossup. It was according to where it landed. Usually his sister, Gina's because her birthday came a few days before mine. So he wanted to celebrate Easter at her house for our birthdays. My Mom and Dad would usually visit for my birthday until my Dad couldn't…

The next day, September 17, 1999, we woke up to his father yelling up the stairs saying he could use some help: "I got a little bit of water in the basement and I need some help".

So I got up and made coffee, and Rob rolled over while he was waiting for it. We didn't look outside yet because it was still dark out. It was around 5:00 in the morning.

9/17/1999… 9+ (1+7)+(1+9+9+9) =9… end of a time … major change to come, according to numerology. (In numerology, and in most cases, you add all the numbers until you get to a single digit.) I was also practicing with tarot cards… the tower card came up in a few spreads I did…not a good card…

I gave Rob his coffee and he slowly got up, got dressed and went down stairs. He said he heard sloshing so he opened the basement door.

I heard him yell "Pop a little bit of water? This is not a little bit of water!"

When I looked outside, by this time the sun had come up enough to where I could see, there was a lake of water outside of our house. We could not see the hedges for the house across the street that were 3 feet high. They were submerged. There was water everywhere, and 4 ½ feet of water in the basement. *A little bit a water, huh, Pop?* He said he woke up to his mattress floating around.

Since Rob and I took over the mortgage payments and utility bills we moved upstairs out of the basement and into the master bedroom and Jim moved to the basement. One of his quirks was he always kept the plastic on the mattress so when the water came up in the basement the plastic kept him from sinking… and possibly saved his life.

The two younger boys got moved from the other room in the basement where Kalan and I would sing lullabies and Ryan would be in his crib listening with his right hand in his diaper and his left hand holding his bottle…*like Ed O'Neill's character "Ed Bundy" in Fox's show "'Married… with Children"*. They got moved to the smaller back room and the older 2 took over Gina's room when she got married and moved out.

I do love her very much but two adult Aries women in the same house... not a good idea. We get along great and are good friends but we just can't live together.

My washer and dryer ended up somewhere in the middle of the other part of the basement. And the spare refrigerator… ended up in yet another part of the basement and had tipped over. All the food we had just bought fell into the contaminated water… and… the electric was still on. The power company hadn't cut the power until two days later. So he could've been electrocuted.

Good thing they both had rubber waders for fishing... they came in quite handy. Rob got his waders on and went to the basement to rescue as much of his step father's computer equipment and electronics as he could.

Bound Brook was one big lake. Most of our stuff was still in the shed from the apartment. We lost everything that was in it. Everything... including the piano I taught myself how to play the song "Doe a Deer" from the movie "The Sound of Music" on, and Rob sometimes used it to write music.

The water was contaminated and about four feet everywhere. The shed was five feet high and to the roof was another two feet high. We were on High St., so it wasn't a flood zone therefore we did not have flood insurance. It wasn't covered. Everything in that shed was destroyed. Everything we had out there… was gone.

With Rob, being the way he was, everyone else came first. After the water receded a bit, he and his brother were in the driveway checking the damage on one of the basement windows when they saw the neighbors across the street getting ripped off by someone charging them to help get the water out of their basement. So they decided they were going to help people as volunteers.

The two of them went and helped other people get water from their basements first while we still had four and a half feet of water in our basement. We could wait. Chrissy, Troy's wife, stayed and helped me with the kitchen and stuff at the house. Not really much we could do but I would have been lost without her. She kept me focused and we got a lot done.

We sent Jacob to my Mom and Dad's in Waretown by Barnegat Bay, and Rob's sister, Gina, picked up Kalan and Ryan and took them to my mother in law's who took them to stay with Rob's youngest sister, Trish, in Florida. Bandjo, our oldest, was stranded in Manville which was like an island at the time.

My boys were split up, most of our stuff was destroyed, my 1988 Chevy Celebrity wagon, and his 1968 Ford Bronco were in the driveway with water up to their doors. Water everywhere and my husband was out with his younger brother, Troy, helping a lot of other people.

Everyone says Rob is such a great guy! Where was he when I needed him?! Not there. He was really never there when I needed him. Yup Rob is such a great guy. I am so glad he was able to help you.

For three days he and Troy helped people clear out their basements until the fourth day when the building inspector told them they had to stop because of black mold and structure damage in the houses.

We didn't leave the house because we weren't evacuated. After the second day the power company cut the power so we cooked on the grill and used flashlights. Just like camping. Just the four of us… no big deal.

About a week later, Rob started showing signs of what he thought was Legionaries Disease, because of the mold in the basements he was in, so he went and got checked out. While he was there he told the doctor he had woken up on the floor at work one day and doesn't know why. All the tests came up negative; thank goodness he just developed a bit of bronchitis. Nothing serious, however she did order a CT scan.

That is when we found out about the monster growing in his head.

An AVM… An "arteriovenous malformation" which is arteries in the brain going straight to the veins instead of feeding capillaries which feed the cells… it built a monster in his head the size of two golf balls side by side… the Neurosurgeon said it was the largest he had ever seen…

CHAPTER 6

ROBERT AND THE MONSTER

Rob, a memory of what he looked like when we first started dating

Our first Christmas together Rob playing a friend's guitar just before he got sick

Usually when people were there he would put on a show for them so they could say "what a great guy". But when I became more of a nurse for him it became even harder and eventually I was hoping Robert was still in there and would come back to me.

But he never did. Once in a while I would get a glimpse - but just a glimpse.

For some reason Sascha popped in my head today. I haven't thought about him in a while. He was the "Adopt a Cop" in the school district my boys went to when they were little. Boy did I have a crush on him… 6'4" tall, dark hair, military buzz fade cut, blue azure eyes, clean shaved, boyish face, perfect body, beautiful smile, absolutely gorgeous! And a sweetheart of a guy. Protector type. Every mom at the event had a crush on him. About 6 ½ years younger than me… just into his 30's.

When I worked at the High School as a paraprofessional class room aide, I got to know him and worked with him on occasion. He told me when his wife left him but did not tell me why. So he was single for a while. I found out his birthday is at the end of September, and he is a Libra on the end of the Virgo cusp… I am very big on birthdays so I make it a point to find these things out and I always make it a point to say happy birthday. (Libra is my opposite.)

Every year since I met Sascha I have always sent him a birthday wish. Always. I send him holiday greetings as well. I used to send him updates on Rob and the boys just to keep in contact.

Then I stopped because he was not my friend anymore. He was Rob's friend. I had to watch what I said to him and everyone that knew Rob. I used to confide in Sascha because I thought he was my friend.

While I was on a walk and he was in a cruiser he would stop and say hello and ask how things were. He also called once in a while to ask how things were going. He always had his number blocked so it would come up "anonymous".

But he wasn't. He wasn't telling me things anymore like he used to. It was like he only told me things to get my confidence. We weren't conversing like we used to. He was now one of Rob's buds and I had lost yet another friend.

That is what happens with a narcissist. They make it so they are the perfect person to everyone else. No one sees what they are really like. They keep you isolated so you don't have any one to talk to. No friends. They praise you to their friends but don't let you say anything or allow you to talk to anyone.

For a while he started calling again but only to find out how Rob was, so I stopped confiding in him and would just update him on Rob's illness. I would just send an email when Rob started declining and then another when he died. Sascha and a few other officers that knew Rob plus the rescue workers came to Rob's funeral but I really didn't get to talk to them… it's the last time I saw them. They came in, paid their respects, and left.

The last time I spoke with Sascha, was the day after Rob's death was announced in the newspaper. He came by to make me aware of a guy trying to take custody of Rob's 9mm that he left me. *The same guy that convinced Rob to sign my mustang, Irene, over to him also convinced him to sign his Sig Sauer over to him and he went to the cop shop to collect it. Well we needed to put a stop to this right away.*

Scott was "Jonny on the spot" with a pink slip signed by Rob, signing his gun over to the very same thief that stole my Mustang and it took two years to get her back. Sascha had called me and asked if I knew anything about it. Of course I told Sascha I didn't. *"Oh Rob what did you do now?"* I had to look at the paperwork.

I looked in the safe at what I had and lo and behold there were some papers in there with Rob's signature signing his gun over to Scott's father. But… thank God the guy didn't have a leg to stand on. Rob's social security number was wrong and Rob's Will overrides the guy's word… and the pink slip is void.

Rob left everything to me in a will he made up and had notarized before he got really bad. He knew I would make sure it would go where it needed to go and I wouldn't be selfish. He did do the best he could. He wasn't a total jerk. He was a pretty good guy most of the time when he was sober and when he started working with the computer companies, he was sober most of the time...

Until he got sick and started on the medications. Then his personality changed again…

Some would say Rob had three personalities. There was Bandjo, or "Bandji", the Dale family called him… the original personality. This was the one everyone loved. The one that played guitar and was musically inclined and an all-around good person with integrity and talent. The guy I fell in love with. The guy I married.

Rob was the intelligent workaholic. Still a bit talented and worked hard. Then there was Bob. The other guy. The controlling narcissistic, lazy, alcoholic that was abusive and was a completely different person. Even his face would change when Bob came out.

In May 2000, He had a grand mal seizure, then, went into a vegetative state, and my Bandji man disappeared forever... In June 2003, when Rob had that first stroke, the monster "Bob" started to come out more and more. The second stroke is when he started seeing things and his eyes would change. Then the double stroke in December 2004... which took his chord hand... he would never be able to play guitar again... he was 45.

Sometimes, once in a while it almost seemed like my Bandji man was in there... which is why I was able to put up with it for so long. I always had hope. Hope is what kept me going. The medications they put him on also had a lot to do with how he was. First it was Dilantin. He was started on that before the seizure in May of 2000. He was still kind of okay but always worked so I really didn't see much difference in him. He would just come home to sleep.

After that first seizure, he stopped playing his guitars. All these guitars and he just stopped playing...he would try once in a while but would get frustrated because his fingers couldn't find the chords...so he stopped.

In 2003, after the first stroke, they added more seizure meds. That's when Bob showed up. Keppra was the worst. He was on the Dilantin and Keppra when he grabbed me by the throat and started squeezing because I said the word "Epilepsy" instead of "seizure disorder". His brother, Troy, came in the room at just the right moment and he let go. The doctors at St. Peter's Hospital would not allow me to visit because I "upset him". I had to stay out of his room until we got to JHN in Philadelphia, Jefferson Hospital for Neuroscience.

I upset him... not the medication but me. All I did was tell him what the doctor said... but I upset him.

But In January of 2004, Bob overtook what was left of Rob and I had to deal with that monster for 12 more years. *I mourned my Robert for 12 years.* People did not understand what I had to deal with. Bandji and Rob were gone and I was left with Bob! But I had to take it. Vows... "through sickness and health"... I promised and I cannot break my promises, even if it takes my whole life. A sacrifice. I would have to stay no matter what.

He was on Keppra when he beat Ryan at 12 years old for coming down the stairs with a smile on his face... it would be the last time Ryan dared to smile again... My Boo Bear was afraid to smile...

Every time he had a seizure they would increase the Keppra. Each time they increased it Robert became more and more abusive to me and the boys. I could take whatever I got but the boys... I was not having it. That is when I insisted they get him off the Keppra. It was the medication making him abusive, not him.

Another reason I stayed... hope to find the right medication so I could have my Robert back. I just kept the boys away from him so he couldn't hurt them anymore.

In January 2004 when he had the second stroke, he was so different, even people in the hospital were different around him. Not as friendly. It seemed like they didn't want to be in the same room with him. Like he got cold and dark all of a sudden. At first, he didn't seem too bad but as time went by and medications increased, his personality got worse. My sister called him "Bob".

I remember it like it just happened and it stays fresh in my mind. The day he had that second stroke. It was January 21, 2004. The seizure wouldn't stop. They worked on him for what seemed like forever. The last time I saw him have a seizure was when I lost my Bandji... now he was having a grand mal seizure that took 10 ml of Ativan to knock down. Any more than that would have killed him.

His youngest sister, Trish, stayed with me in the hallway as I broke down and melted to the floor.

I knew deep down he was going to change again...

Then the hallucinations started...

He shouted, "Look! It's the bugle boy on the ceiling! Do you see him? Look El! There he goes!" following something he was pointing to on the ceiling as it went toward the window.

Unfortunately, he did change.... It seemed like once he came back they couldn't get rid of him fast enough.

When he went for his follow up appointment a week later, the neurologist told him he couldn't work anymore... he was mortified. He worked hard all his life and finally had his dream job, and now... he couldn't.

A workaholic not allowed to work… he finally had his dream job and couldn't do it anymore…

For the next few months he would be going to rehab to build up his strength and get back to doing things with the boys and would do side work. Then he would have a seizure that would knock him down again. Each time he had a seizure they put him in the hospital, then three days later, send him home. And he would have to go to rehab to build up again. His personality would get worse each time.

Finally, while at the hospital I was talking to one of the rehab techs. She told me he needed to be in a facility for "intense" rehab which was about three to six weeks. He used to call these places "Old Folks Homes" but when he was put into one, we saw that it is not just old people but all ages. He would talk to everyone there and I would get a bit of a break. He still wanted me there all the time but at least he had someone else to keep him occupied until I got there.

When he was at these facilities, I could go home at night and get a bit of reprieve from his constant demanding me to go get this or go do that. *Get me this. Get me that. Get the nurse. Fix the bed. Get me food… That's how he spoke to me. I just did what I was told… like a robot following program.*

Every time I mentioned I wanted to visit my Mom and Dad, he would have another seizure preventing me from going. My Dad was sick and put in rehab places in Forked River then Barnegat. Rob wouldn't let me go to see my Dad. He kept me close because he was "afraid" to be left alone. By this time all the visitors stopped coming. I was all he had left. Then the hallucinations were getting worse.

In Somerset Hospital with one of the hallucinations, he saw people coming out of the closet marked for their organs and he ran out with the IV port still in his wrist, just after midnight, he ran out of the hospital. I had to go pick him up and bring him home. I had already taken my medication and was almost asleep when the hospital called me and told me I needed to come get him.

Thank God it was only Somerset Hospital… 10 minutes away and straight up the street. I met them in front of the main entrance lobby. Then took him home after they removed the port from his wrist… he told me about the hallucination on the way home… and started talking about conspiracies… paranoia had set in…

The next day I had to call the insurance company and explain what happened. He needed to be in a hospital but he would not go back to Somerset this time. It was back to JHN in Philly…a two and a half hour drive plus tolls and paying for parking plus the hotel room for me and his Mom… she met us at JHN. One of many trips.

Rita and I had become very close. I don't think I could have gotten through a lot of it without her.

I finally got to visit my Dad in late August at the rehab place in Barnegat. My Mom and I picked up a chili dog with onions for him on the way. His face lit up like a Christmas tree when he saw us. He was smiling ear to ear. He had me order a special pair of shoes from a catalog he had. As my mom and I left him, he was riding his cart to see us out like he always did with company. He was happy just to see us.

That was the last time I was able to hug my father… he never got to wear those shoes.

That night, when I got home, it was late and I knew I had to get up to go back to the JFK Rehabilitation Center where Rob was first thing in the morning. I no sooner walked it the door a just little after 11:00 PM, when the phone rang… Rob had a grand mal seizure. I had to go to Metuchen, where he was, to take care of him. He wouldn't let anyone else near him.

After driving 5 hours round trip to visit with my mom and dad, and being exhausted from the day, I had to drive another 50 minutes to Metuchen.

In September, 2004, Rob was still in the rehab hospital in Metuchen. My father was moved to Southern Ocean County Hospital. His gall bladder had perforated and needed immediate surgery. Rob wouldn't let me go to be with my Dad. I needed to be there and he wouldn't let me go.

Finally, a little over a week later, Rob allowed me to see my Dad. I had been talking with the nurse when she saw my face. She asked what was wrong and I told her about my Dad and how I couldn't leave Rob. She said he would be fine and I should go. Rob finally let me because the nurse was there. So I left before he could change his mind, and finally got to see him.

When I got to my Dad, he was on a respirator and they made us wear gowns and gloves. He had become toxic from the bile that seeped out from the perforation.

The most huggable man in the world and we couldn't touch him.

He was awake but couldn't talk. All he could do was use his eyes to communicate. He taught me a long time ago how to know what people were really saying by their eyes. He was thirsty but all he could have was a "lolli pop" sponge dipped in ice water to wet his lips and tongue. We had to be careful not to let the sponge drip because it would cause him to choke from the respirator.

My sister and I stayed as long as they would allow us to. My Mom wouldn't let us touch him even with the gloves on because he would wince every time she tried. She didn't want us to hurt him.

When the doctor came in to talk with us he said Daddy would be able to eat whatever he wanted when he got better and is able to go home. I promised him I would make him his favorite T-bone steak with gravy, and Sandy said all the mashed potatoes and corn on the cob he wants. (He always liked corn on the cob but he would get sick when he tried to eat it.)

Then I got another call from the rehab facility… Rob had a seizure. I had to rush back. Found out when I got there it was a focal seizure, but I had to stay overnight with him from then on. He was finally released at the end of September.

Three people passed within a month. First, on my sister's son's birthday, September 9, 2004 her mother in law passed. Then my cousin Tracy passed a couple weeks later. She had spina bifida. My Dad would dance with her in her wheel chair. Her funeral was October 1st…my niece, Shannon's birthday.

My Aunt Marlene was told she wouldn't live past 6 months… she was 44 when she decided she had enough and just stopped fighting. She died September 27, 2004… just before her 45th birthday.

The day after Tracy's funeral, around 9:00 AM, I got a call from my big brother Butch. Daddy took a turn for the worst. We needed to get there now.

After the boys got dressed and I got Rob ready, I had the boys put the wheelchair in the van. It was a 2 hour drive down the parkway… we didn't get there until after 1 PM.

That's when my brother, Butch, took me aside and told me: "he's gone El".

My Daddy was gone…

When it was our turn to go in to see him, he was still warm to the touch. His fever spiked to 106 when he died during the night. He was 77.

While we were getting his service in order, we were sent to the florist. Momma only wanted a single red rose from her. Nothing else. We wanted to give him something too. While we were in the parking lot saying goodbye, my brother Ray's wife, Nancy felt left out because we weren't consulting with her. She wanted a casket blanket of flowers.

She loved him as if he were her own father too. Everyone loved him… after all he was Santa Claus… He was the one people turned to for help… "CCC – Call Cal Collect… he always answered the call".

That's when it hit me like a solid punch in the chest. I thought I was having a heart attack. Butch was Captain of the Manville Rescue Squad at the time. He caught me as I fell back. He checked me out right there and found I was ok.

He said it was an anxiety attack… that's what they are like… the doctor confirmed it.

Later, My Mother in Law, Rita, helped when she went to the doctor's with me and she had the doctor put me on Xanax for anxiety.

I was kept on Xanax for a few years until it stopped working, then switched to Ativan (Lorazepam) which I still have, but only take as needed. It slows the heart rate which raises when you are stressed. Since my heart goes faster than it is supposed to anyway, they kept me on it to slow it down.

It also slows your metabolism. The migraine preventive/anti-depressant medicine, Nortriptyline, I was on raises you heart beat and makes you gain weight by causing cravings and stress eating.

Starting early in December 2004, Rob started having seizures back to back… they were killing him. He was having multiple seizures in a day. That's when they found where the seizures were coming from. Of course the seizures were stemming from where I said they were coming from…

The right front temporal lobe of his brain… which is where the AVM is…and the last two strokes he had. The AVM was killing him. They needed a machine to tell them that… a $20,000.00 a day test… Common sense told me…for free.

We always hoped he would pick up his guitars and start playing them again but on December 09, 2004, the double stroke took his left hand…

the chord hand… he would never be able to play again. After that he no longer stood tall… he was always slumped over. He was totally different. This would be the first of many Christmas's and special days he spent in the hospital…

Two mandolins, a banjolin, a banjo, 16 guitars, (10 of which he kept right there in our bedroom) and various equipment, and he couldn't play any of them ever again. The one thing about him I loved the most, and he couldn't do it anymore.

One of my biggest regrets… all that recording equipment, but no recordings of him playing by himself. He wasn't playing as much when he worked in Jersey City but then completely stopped playing when he started working as Director of Communications with Answernet, one of the largest telephony companies in the world… he was never home to play…

Robert was indeed a good man with integrity. After all he had an honorable discharge from being in the army for 6 years. He talked about it a lot. Wrote songs about his experiences and played beautifully on the guitar that mesmerized me every time he played. I could listen to him for hours.

Unfortunately there are no good recordings of him playing. Just the one his youngest sister, Trish, put in the memorial video and on YouTube ...but has kids talking and playing in the background.

He had a touch that was like no other... magic. But when he came home after that second stroke, he was *different.* Even the sex was different. I felt like I was cheating and I just started holding back. I used to put everything I had in it and take the pain of it for as long as it took because that is what an Aries does. We give it our all. But when it is gone, it is gone.

As time went on, I went through the motions and did what was expected of me. And after 8 years of being with this stranger… I just couldn't bring myself to do those wifely duties anymore, *especially when he started sexting his old girlfriend from his pre-army days over the next 4 years.*

The entities here keep saying and pointing these certain things out to me…

Rob was supposed to die on May 29, 2000… when he had that first grand mal seizure…

5 + 2 + 9 + 2 + 0 + 0 + 0 = 9 end of a time…

January 21, 2004… the stroke that changed Rob…

1+2+1+2+0+0+4=1 begin a new time…

Daddy died October 2, 2004… between Shannon and Ryan's birthdays.

1 + 0 + 2 + 2+0 +0 +4 = 9 end of a time…
December 9, 2004… Rob's double stroke
1+2+9+2+0+0+4 = 9 end of a time…
October 25, 2015… The day Rob's vessel gave out…
1+0+2+5+2+0+1+5 = 7? Luck? Hmm…what does this mean?

Balial Baraciele (Babs)
You will find out soon enough Ellen… get back to the story.

CHAPTER 7

A FORCE OF HIS OWN

Getting ready for work with the morning sun and beautiful blue sky…

Dave from a picture of him on a roof top

Pretty sad…

The ones that care enough to call you every day are the ones you are supposed to stay away from because they are the bad ones.

The good ones don't call, they are already taken, or they just plain don't exist.

That is why we end up with the bad ones.
We are tired of being alone.
So we suffer in silence or alone.
We end up with the cards we are dealt and we have to play them or fold.
2003

This is a letter I wrote to Rob before he had his first stroke...

It is time to face facts. A man who only finds fault and resentment towards someone he says he loves-does not. You always look for things to be angry at me for. The littlest thing would erase everything I have done that was right. Are you looking for an excuse to get rid of me? Or are you trying to make me make the decision to go so you don't look like the bad guy. If I do go, who will rub your feet or wash and iron your clothes or cook your food or remind you to take your pills or pick up after you? Especially when all you do is criticize and order me around and tell me I can't have this or that. Everything is "NO you can't have it" "What are you making for dinner" "Get my clothes". No "please" or "thank you" or "Honey would you mind"... No. YOU DEMAND IT. I am nothing more than a servant that you can't stand. I am not "allowed" to have things or do things. If I do I get resentment or a cold silent treatment. You don't care how much you hurt me. I don't matter. I am not allowed to say anything. I am ordered to "shut the F up". When you do talk to me you talk at me like I am a child or stupid jackass retard that can't possibly understand anything. You constantly remind me I am too stupid to hold a real job. I can only hold a meaningless job at minimum wage. I couldn't possibly get a job with any kind of importance. If I did I wouldn't be allowed to stay the hours you do. Only you are allowed to have a job that requires your time. For instance; it was ok for you to stay late at the Food Bank but when I did I couldn't possibly be working. I must be doing something else. I am tired of having to defend myself even when I have done nothing wrong. I am tired of the accusing looks and the tone in your voice. How could you think like that unless you don't love me and are looking for a way out. I would never nor could I ever do anything like that but yet you are convinced that I would at any given moment. I am sorry but I did make a vow that I would only have you and I would only love you until the day we die and that hasn't changed nor will it ever. But I can't take the way you have been towards me anymore. I have been loyal to you since the day we started dating. You were the one that would stay out and get drunk after work. You were the one that never wanted to come home to me. I was always there – waiting for you. I am not capable of anything. You always accuse me of lying. You think I am a hypochondriac. I am just a machine that doesn't get tired, don't have feelings, can't possibly get sick, but I do get sick and I do get tired and I do hurt. But as long as you get what you want you don't care. I am nothing more than a "fat lazy stupid bitch". Well, you win. I will stay out of your way. You will not have to look at me anymore. I will sleep on the couch and if you walk into a room I will go somewhere else. I will stay out of your way. You have shown me how you feel about me. You never try to make up. You just assume everything is fine – even when it is not. To you the television is more important than our relationship. I am never important to you, only other people are important. I don't matter to you. God forbid you should be inconvenienced or you should have to wait for anything. I've been waiting forever it seems for you to love me half as much as I love you but I have come to terms with that now. You will never love me or have ever really loved me. You just don't like change and you needed me at one time and now I am nothing more than a habit to you. All I ever wanted was for you to love me. Now I know that will never be. For 20 years that is all I hoped for but for 20 years you have shown me you would never love me. I was just too blind and naive to see it. I miss the way you used to hold me and I longed for it. I miss your touch. I miss the man that once loved me back and wanted me. I wish you could be nice to me like you are with other people. But I only get your mean side. You always talk to me with resentment and then you go to bed like nothing is wrong. Something is wrong. I cannot forget the way you treat me and disregard my feelings. You either need to work with me or there is nothing left. I can't do this alone anymore. I have always been there for you. I don't know what else to do.

I just never gave it to him and he never found it. Instead my boyfriend, Dave, found it in the storage unit while we were going through the boxes to see what we could get rid of.

Dave is a force of his own. I met him shortly after finding out Captain, the soldier I met online, was nothing more than a smooth talking scammer I befriended from Facebook.

We met on one of those dating sites on line... *OK Cupid.com to be precise.* He lived in Bristol, Pa. Right down I-95, halfway to Philadelphia. About 20-25 minutes away. He was 49 at the time (I was 55) and is everything I was NOT looking for. But his pickup line... "Too bad you live so far away". I googled the distance and said "it isn't that far, only about half an hour". The rest is history.

Our first date was January 15th 2017 at Oxford Valley Mall in Lehigh Valley, Pa. I picked him up at his place and we talked in the car on the way.

His eyes were so crystal blue they sparkled. I could get lost in them forever… He seemed really cool. Clean shaved and buzz cut hair. He smelled really good and looked nice. He was looking for Sub-Way but they were gone so we ended up having Chinese at the food court and then walked around the mall a bit. As we walked we talked… we seemed to hit it off well.

He wasn't as tall as he said he was and the angle of the pictures made him look… *only about 5' 7" as opposed to 5' 10"*… but he stood tall and straight, very handsome, and well kept. When he took off his jacket, the muscles… wow… solid and… wow.

I had only lost 70 pounds and still had another 50 pounds to go. I was afraid as soon as he saw me I would never hear from him again. I just kept my jacket on so he wouldn't see.

When we got out to the car, we talked some more and talked about the tattoos we each have. I have a hummingbird with a ribbon for autism and my children's names on the middle of my back, and an eagle in flight with my children's colors and wind with the words "Fly Free" on my right shoulder blade. He has his name on his right arm and the outline of a scorpion on his chest. He slapped himself where the tattoos are located to show me where they are… kind of abrupt.

When I went to reach for the Garmin to set it to take him home he reached for it as well and said "you don't need that I know how to get home".

The mount for it fell out of the car never to be seen again. I didn't notice until after I dropped him off and went to reach for it to set it for home.

For our second date, a few weeks later, he helped me and two of my brothers - Butch and Kenny, my sister Sandy and her husband Len, Kenny's younger daughter, Shannon and her husband, Shane, and Sandy's son, Josh and his fiancée, Alicia. Everyone lived over an hour away but they took the time to help me… it was a lot just arranging this…

My big brother Butch, as soon as he saw Dave, he said: "not him". But Dave was helping me after only meeting me once so I couldn't understand why. Maybe it was the way he was dressed or maybe he saw something I had missed but Butch did not want me to date him.

I was behind on my storage unit payment so the gate rejected my code. I went inside to talk to the girl about arranging payments but she said she needed at least half. Butch paid it for me without a second thought.

While we were loading the pickup trucks and getting the stuff out of the unit the girl came and said we have to come up with the other half or put the stuff back in the unit.

Again big brother Butch came to the rescue. He put it on his other credit card and whispered to me: "don't tell Susan". He really didn't have the money but he bailed me out anyway. It is the way we were raised.

My Dad was like that. He would give you the shirt off his back if you needed it.

After emptying the storage unit in Green Brook, we headed to the storage units in Lawrenceville another hour away. We loaded the units and came back to my apartment for lunch. I had homemade chicken vegetable soup and cookies and brownies for everyone. We also had fruit and sandwiches with homemade bread.

One thing I can do is cook and bake. My mother always taught us how to be a good hostess.

Dave really liked the soup. It is one thing when family tells you it is good, but a whole different meaning when someone you hardly know likes your cooking. I set up a quart for him to take home.

We kept in touch mostly texting with emoji's and stuff while he was waiting for the bus to go home from work, and when he was on the bus he would text some more, and we got to know each other a little more and talked a lot.

Some of the emoji's were the monkey faces. And others were just crazy…

He said his favorite books as a child was "Curious George and The Man with the Yellow Hat" by H. A. Rey.

And on our third date he came over and helped me pack some stuff up to take to the storage unit. All he wanted was beer, chicken wings, and a TV to see the football game.

When I picked him up we stopped and got him a 6 pack of Budweiser Tall Boys, then I went to Costco to get chicken wings for us to cook while he got acquainted with the boys and watched the game. He gave me a $20.00 bill and told me to get a big jug of water and two bags of chicken wings.

While I was in Costco, I double checked my wallet to see if I had enough money, the $20.00 he gave me wasn't there. I lost a $20.00 bill from my apartment to my car and from my car to Costco. I could swear I put it in my wallet but it was gone. I had just enough in my account for one bag of chicken wings and could not get the water.

I could see he was angry but he kept his composure and just made due with what I got. He took half the bag and made the hot wings in the pot on the stove and I took the other half and made the sweet BBQ sauce ones in the slow cooker. I used my rice cooker and made rice to go with it, then used my frying pan to crisp them up a bit. They came out phenomenal and he ended up staying with me overnight.

He mentioned: "This seems like a really nice place. I could live in a place like this."

I said: Um, yeah, ok" a little puzzled. I took him back to his place and all was well.

That was February 18, 2017. He disappeared when I told him I was fine after I went to the doctor for a check-up. It went from calling and texting three or four times a day to nothing. Not a word.

Not long after the Captain had been trying to play more head games on me and Dave disappeared, I had a bout with Seasonal Depression Disorder where in winter I get really bad and I feel like no one wants to be bothered with me.

Everyone leaves. Rob was gone. Dave left. Then the Captain left. No friends at the time. Family was too busy to talk. Jacob kept having seizures on a daily basis and grand mal seizures almost every week, and

Ryan stayed in his room all the time. I was alone. Dark and cold… I fell into a very dark place.

Finally Dave responded and on Sunday March 12th, he told me to come get him. So we got back together. I should have left him alone. But I picked him up and we went shopping and got some food and he bought some flowers for me when I wasn't looking, then we went to Joe's liquor store and picked up some beer, red hots cinnamon whiskey, vodka and some wine coolers and headed to my apartment and partied up.

He drank a lot of beer. We also did vodka shots and were having a great time. After dinner we went in my room and talked… a lot. He told me things I don't think I was ready to hear but he needed to tell. He was sitting in my father's rocking chair looking lost... I had to help him. I knelt on the floor in front of him and that is when he looked at me with tears in his eyes… so broken.

For some reason people tell me things they wouldn't tell anyone else; their deepest darkest secrets. Why? I don't know. But when I looked into his eyes I saw something in this man's soul that has been haunting him for a long time and he needed to get it out. This man has more than just one or two demons to deal with... he has many. The torment he has been going through is more than any one man should have to deal with. But these memories haunt him every time he stops to take a break. So he starts drinking as soon as he can to make the demons in his head go away.

In the morning, around 4:00 A.M he jumped up like a pop tart pastry out of a toaster, fully dressed and ready to start the day. I was just finally falling asleep and he wanted to get up and go. I started calling him "Pop Tart" from then on.

He was supposed to go to work the next day but he directed me to the back door of a liquor store in Bristol instead of where we were supposed to go. He said "give me a minute." When he came back he got in the car and guzzled downed three big 20 ounce beers in the parking lot before texting his boss about the snow storm coming that he was supposed to get the plows ready for. Three Budweiser Tall Boys in less than five minutes. Between each gulp he looked at me like he saw something that scared the hell out of him and took another big swig as if to make what he was seeing go away.

It was 7:00 AM… why was a liquor store open at 7:00 in morning…

I had to get gas so he directed me to a gas station and talked to his boss while we were there and they told him: "don't come in drunk".

He got in the car and made me take him home with me. At the time I wasn't quite sure of what was going on and I didn't know where I was. I did not know him and I was now afraid of him. I don't like being afraid.

In the morning he woke me up demanding more beer... at 5:00 in the morning. Which I thought was strange but I didn't know what to think and hadn't had my coffee yet and I don't function very well without my coffee. The liquor store doesn't open until 10.

This started a week long binge. Every time I tried to take him back to his place he would get extremely agitated and plead with me not to take him back. My car is not that big and with the top up, I am quite claustrophobic. He was forceful and very loud and back at my apartment I needed to keep the peace. He kept promising he would stop and this will be the last trip to the liquor store and he will go home tomorrow.

He would only get a couple of beers at a time but would make me take him to get more when he ran out… he even took money from my change jars to buy his beer. When the liquor store closed he made me take him to bars and wait in the car for him… it was Rob all over again…

What I didn't know was the house he was living at is a recovery house for drug addicts and alcoholics who are trying to get clean. Since he had been drinking, he couldn't go back drunk. If he did, he would be kicked out and put on the street. That's how they work. If you fall off the wagon you are out. No slip ups, no second chance. You're done.

This nightmare lasted for an entire week. It finally came to an end on March 18, 2017.

How was he moved into my apartment April 2nd? I don't know. But he called me the day after my 56th birthday and had me pick him up at a pizza place in Bristol and the next thing I knew he was moving in. He said he wouldn't drink. I didn't know they served beer at the pizza place and when I got there he already had two.

Three weeks later my niece, Connie and her 13 year old son moved in. And by June 2nd Pop Tart moved out and I came home with a bruise on my face and a broken cheek bone.

CHAPTER 8

THE STONES ... AND WHAT LIES WITHIN

Stones set up with the help of "Owen"

Each stone is different in its own way. No two are alike. And they all have a secret. Some have more than one.

Connie always wore this amethyst amulet wrapped in wire on a black chord around her neck along with another choker and it kind of caught my eye. I just admired it. One day we were in my room talking and the subject came up and she took it off and asked it a question silently and the thing moved... all by itself... her hand didn't move but the amulet did. *Whoa... cool...*

"How did you do that?" I asked.

She explained about energy. "Everything has energy".

And it all made sense.

Everything has energy... I mean what is a rock made out of? Molecules. Molecules are made from atoms, atoms have protons, neutrons, electrons and what do those little things do? They all race around a nucleus with what is called "energy". Everything has energy. It is all around us, everywhere. You just don't see it. Wow. Got it. Now it makes sense. To me that is. But to explain it... good luck with that.

When Sandy came to visit in June 2017 after Dave moved out, we went to the mall and looked around a bit to cheer me up. Connie kept steering us to this one fantasy store she wanted me to go in. They have all kinds of Spiritual stuff in there! Fairies and dragons and steampunk, skulls, dream catchers, rocks, pendulums, and Tarot cards and Chi stuff and you name it they got it... they even have clothes. We walked in there and I felt like I was in my dream land! Like I really needed to be there!

After looking around a bit, Connie picked up this beautiful dark blue onyx pendulum which swung a little for her but when she put it over my hand it went nuts! Like it was meant for me. So she and my sister chipped in and they got it for me. And that is when I met "them" for the first time.

I downloaded instructions on how to use a pendulum and how to practice with it and fine tune it and work with it so it will work accurately with its owner and I followed the directions every day. It said it takes about a month but it only took a day or two for it to work for me with very high accuracy... so I thought...

His name was Owen.

As of January 22, 2018 I have decided to get back to writing my book. Starting with notes and see where I can get my book back in order.

Today was also the first full day of not smoking because I made a promise to God I will quit and well you do not break a promise to the Lord. After almost 15 years of not smoking I started smoking again in August because Connie would not say no to me.

Also had a CT scan done on my lungs today.... we shall see if the emphysema became active again when the report is done tomorrow.

Nothing showed in the CT scan that wasn't there before. I was lied to by my stone. He lied to me a lot. He told me I had cancer and the nodes in my lungs were growing. He had me convinced I was going to die in a matter of months. He also told me it had spread into my head and that's what was causing the headaches and nose bleeds.

He also caused me to dream of being captive. In one of those dreams there was a tall slender narcissistic man watching my every move and controlling me. When I woke up I asked him if he was the man I was dreaming about and he said yes. He was trying to control me. He no longer worked for me and he even said goodbye to me.

His name was Owen. He first told me his name was Oye. He is the spirit in my blue onyx pendulum. On the other end of the chain was a blue aquamarine Chakra ball which also has a spirit.

He first told me his name was Ilfy... found out it is an acronym I L F Y ... when I found out what it meant I wouldn't talk to him for a long time. When I did start talking to him again he finally told me his name is Al and he was from England.

Oye finally told me his name is actually Owen and he was from Scotland. Which is why the two didn't get along and the chain would always have a knot in it no matter how many times I untied it, I would always find it knotted again. So I allowed them to have the one knot and they were happy with that.

It was my first pendulum and I didn't know much about them except it would answer my questions and circled the letters on the notepad app I have on my phone. It was quite peculiar to me how it went in the opposite directions the instructions said, but it worked so I never gave it much thought. I thought it did that because I am left handed. It also circled the words it wanted to use and it told me all kinds of things. He would also help me find things on the internet.

He was very much into Science and Math. Binary code was big for him. He was trying to teach me how it worked but I had other things to do and what he wanted took hours. I had to stop so I could cook dinner and do mom things.

He would tell me when there was a new spirit in the apartment and we would find stones on our walks to put the spirits in. Problem is when there was something he had to tell me about the spirit it was usually in Spanish or another language and I had to figure out how to translate it. I also had to figure out who the spirit came for.

He taught me a lot of things and showed me things I never knew existed; for instance…

One time, we were looking up some things on the internet, when he took me to a hidden site on Google. It was an archive I would never have found on my own. But what it had was information about God and Powerful spells with Hebrew writing and the 72 names of God and His Angels and pages of information on stuff I never knew anything about.

This was stuff you don't learn about in Sunday school or church… or anywhere for that matter. It was technically the Science of God and everything He is… including how to use His power to make things happen.

Another time he brought me to certain rocks in the fantasy store in the malls. At Oxford Valley Mall, we got Dave some rocks and a selenite bar to put them on. While we were there, this big white Celestial Crystal stone caught my attention and I had to get it. I took Dave home and helped him set up his rocks then went home and added the Celestial stone to my collection. That was the first time I heard it "talk"… w*icked…*

It was a soft gentle man's voice and barely audible but it called my name. I did the research and found why it is called a "Celestial stone". According to a few websites, angels can talk to you through it. Owen said it was the Archangel, Gabriel, calling to me.

As this stone was breaking up, the "Faye" started coming to "help" and they would use the stones to reside in. Owen had me picking up more rocks here and there and somehow I ended up with over 70 stones that I would have to place every day. Then he would have me carry certain stones with me in different pockets; then he wouldn't allow me to take the ones I was supposed to keep with me. Then these "other things" came in and would take over the stones.

He would have me keep the stones in the window for a few days instead of the one night when the moon is completely full. The moon, when full, charges the stones and returns their energy. The salt cleanses them and removes the negative energy so you can reprogram and replace it with positive energy. I found out later from a "Faye" the dark side hurts them… even if it is just a sliver.

I had no idea; I just did what Owen told me to do. I was learning and he was teaching. He had opened a few doors in my room that should not have been opened which makes my room very cold – all the time. These doors also allowed certain "things" in my room that should not have been. Kind of the "not so nice beings" of sorts.

Xedael wants to write…

I want light room

She wanted me to move from sitting on the bed to sitting in the rocking chair by the window so we have some sunshine while we are writing. *(Xedael is an 11 year old muse and big sister to Xedeousrel (4) years old and the first one I met… my first muse.)*

Please might you finish the chapter so we can move on…?

Ok Xedael

The Faye told me to put Loki with Owen and get rid of him so I made a containment sigil, put him in a container and put him in storage. He was not safe to just toss or bury. I had to know no one else would find him and use him. He was evil and Loki is with him now.

Along with a couple of other things he picked out that he wanted. A little blue plastic pearl looking thing that he found on the ground and a pink dyed stone he picked out of a rock bin at the Oxford Valley Mall store.

CHAPTER 9

ANGELS ANSWER THE CALL ...OR IS IT?

no explanation needed...

When they first came, the one in my aquamarine pendant said he was Michael... the Archangel, Michael... in my pendant... He said his name was Archangel Michael. He was sent here by God to help me get "back on track" and help me do the "right thing". When they came and revealed themselves, the first thing they did was tell me to get rid of Owen.

The nightmares were getting more frequent and things started happening. Things would appear out of nowhere. And it was getting worse every day. I found myself in a corner holding my head repeating over and over screaming silently so no one else could hear "stop it stop it stop it stop it!!!" over and over again and again… I felt lost and defeated and it hit me like a ton of bricks! I felt like I was swirling into a hole of dark madness.

Is this a nervous breakdown? Am I having a nervous breakdown? No! No! No! This will not do. I don't have the time or the luxury of having a nervous breakdown.

I heard inside my head "Snap out of it El, your kids need you!"

My attention was turned to the light blue pendant on the windowsill. I asked if it was the one calling me.

It said "yes".

I asked "who are you?"

"Michael"

Shock had set in… did I hallucinate or did he just say he was Michael…

When he spoke, he seemed very "commanding" … no nonsense. The feeling I got from him seemed very strong and in control. There was a warm light blue glow to the pendant as I held it while he guided my hands over the letters spelling out what he wanted to say. That's when he took charge and helped me snap out of my attack of anxiety and super depressive state.

About six weeks later, I was doing a spell of some sort that he had me do because I wanted my son to talk to me again since the blow up on Thanksgiving four months before. We worked on the spell almost every day.

For some reason, this one day, I was wearing a tank top with a skull on it that I liked. The amulet "shook" as if frightened.

I was thinking to myself… *Angels do not shake from fear… especially Archangels.*

I confronted the spirit and said "you are not Michael! Who are you?!"

She said "my name is Ultana and I am of the Irish Faye clan. My spirit wolf's name is Faith."

CHAPTER 10

INTRODUCING "THE FAYE"

The face in the red fishing rock.

Spirits. Fickle in a way. Wonderful fascinating deities, the Faye. They say they do not like being referred to as "fairies". They are not what we knew of as children. Nothing like Tinkerbell or Fairy God Mother or the fairies Fauna, Flora and Merriweather, although Maleficent is close… no they were insulted by these comparisons. They have feathers for their wings. They are not like bug wings but like birds or the stereotype angel. Except some have brown wings instead of white. They also each have their own spirit animal… wolf, hawk, eagle, bear, or other types.

The first one we met was Flik…

We were going through the storage unit trying to get rid of some things when I found this rock with solder wire around it used as a fisherman's weight rock in a crab trap. It was reddish and elongated and smooth from being in the water. The wire was made of an iron pewter alloy of some kind soldered around it so he was trapped and couldn't "jump" to another safer rock.

Once we took the wire off, my son took Flik's rock to the forest across the street where Flik was freed. He was so grateful he came back into one of my crystals for a visit. I have many crystals and some are on silver chains. A while later a few of his friends had come to visit that he had sent to help us for helping him.

I had been praying for help or a guide for so long because I felt so lost and on the verge of a nervous breakdown at this point. I had lost so much. I thought they were an answer to my prayers…

Between bill collection agencies calling constantly, trying to recover from being scammed by a smooth talking scammer, too many people living here, my apartment was a mess, my boyfriend criticizing me for not having it spotless, not enough money, and Jacob having grand mal seizures almost every day at this point, on top of focal seizures that were practically constant… it was just a tad overwhelming.

I was able to get Jake on the Medical Marijuana Program because it is legal in NJ for medical purposes and I found a doctor that could prescribe it. Jacob had a focal seizure lasting over two hours right in the Dr. Tsarouhas' office so he knew I wasn't lying about them.

He pushed the appointments through and I was able to get the card fast. But the pharmaceuticals Jake is on doesn't do anything for them. Besides the epilepsy and autism he also has psychotic behavior from the side effects of the medications he is on. We had to find the right combination. I had already lost my husband because of pharmaceutical medications and now I was losing my son.

Finally the marijuana was helping the focal seizures. They had stopped completely. But the grand mal seizures, though not as long, were still there. Instead of lasting 5 or 10 minutes, they were lasting under 2 minutes. But the location and type of the seizures were very dangerous. He has the SUDEP factor. He also loses a chunk of his memory with each seizure. It takes him a long time to recover as well.

The medications he was put on wasn't working.

For those of you who don't know what epilepsy is, I will explain. Epilepsy is Latin for "seizure disorder" which is caused by misfiring messages in the brain. A seizure is when the brain "seizes up" or freezes like an engine without oil... it can't function. Nothing works. A seizure is painful because all the muscles and organs tighten up in spasms at once and there is no control over anything.

Imagine a charlie horse that wakes you up at night that you get in your calf or your toes cramp up... now picture that all through your body in every muscle and organ you have...

The SUDEP factor means **S**udden **U**nexplained **D**eath of **EP**ilepsy. The organs seize as well. The victim will choke on their own phlegm or their heart will go into fibrillation. It is a very serious and scary infliction. And that is just one of his afflictions. Another is his Psychosis caused by the anti-seizure medication he was using. So they put him on anti-anxiety medication as well.

Jacob was always a very quiet sweetheart. He was a good little boy and really never gave me a problem except for the fact that he is autistic and didn't talk until he was almost 5 years old. *His first word was "cold".* He always did what he was asked with a smile and always said "of course".

He and his brothers always took turns bringing me and Rob coffee every morning since Bandjo moved out. Before that Bandjo would bring up the coffee for us and give us a hug on his way out the door for school.

Jacob was always very sweet and loving... until the monster "Bob" took over Rob and made Jake rub his leg constantly even when he told him his hands hurt. The doctors put Jake on the pharmaceuticals that changed him and when he took all the pills to make the monster leave him alone, Rob came out to save him but the damage had already begun.

I had just refilled his medicine so they were full bottles of clonazepam and Cymbalta... 60 of clonazepam and 30 Cymbalta... he took them all...

The mental hospital Jacob was forced to go to (against our will) stopped the pills abruptly which causes seizures and now he has to take anti-seizure medicine for the rest of his life.

They both cause "thoughts of suicide" and "suicidal tendencies"...

Before you take anything... read the warning labels. I made the mistake of trusting the doctors prescribing these medicines at the time. They, too, are human and do make mistakes…

"Trial and Error" is how they find medications for us to take. We are basically just guinea pigs to test on.

There are plenty of other medications; so don't settle for the first thing they give you... research everything! That is why I took up the study of Neuroscience. I also started studying different pharmaceuticals. I found Medical Marijuana is the safest of all of them. AND IT WORKS! God's all natural medicine.

As with any medication, you only need a small amount and the right dosage, along with the right diet… it works.

There is a song by the band, Adema, called "Better Living Through Chemistry". When I heard this song, the message made sense to me loud and clear.

The Laboratories are the "kitchens" the salesmen or "pusher dealers" give free samples to the doctors or "pushers" and the pharmacist "local dealers" sell the drugs. The only difference? They wear a nametag so we "trust" them.

But do we actually know what chemicals they are giving us?

The messages in this song are loud and clear… all you need to do is listen to the words…

"Greed is taking over the hollow heart of healthcare"

Just open your eyes and see it!

CHAPTER 11

COCOA BEANS

Cocoa

12/11/2018
Tuesday 8:34 AM

The TV shut itself off just before Pop Tart called at 8:06 AM to say good morning. Jake brought me coffee in my "Coffee Addict" cup a few minutes later. I gave up on sleeping so I got up, took my morning pills, went to the bathroom, did some exercises, went to the kitchen and got a peach yogurt and a spoon, told Jake to have some cereal, and asked him to clean up the kitchen a bit so I can work in there.

He said he heard voices in Ryan's room. I told him maybe Ryan is watching a video or something. Then I came back to my room and put some granola in the yogurt and asked Raphael if he liked the peach yogurt and coffee.

"The Boss" likes granola and he is the only one that can taste so when I was done he gave Raphael back the control of the bottle.

I usually make Jake eggs in a basket or egg sandwiches or something yum for breakfast. Ryan prefers scrambled eggs in a basket or just with toast. But my cast iron pan that I got from my Dad was not clean and the kitchen is a mess from last night.

When I am up to cleaning I clean it or Ryan will clean the pans for me, but last night I was just too tired from the weekend and I had gone to the store to get a few things needed and with the weather being cold I am in pain most of the time.

I could swear I just saw Cocoa by the stool next to the rocking chair going toward the windowsill but when I looked there was nothing. I still see her shadow a lot. I miss her so much. Every time I have a yogurt she used to lick the yogurt cup clean when I was done and I always gave her last bite of my egg sandwich or turkey sandwich or whatever I had. I always made it "Cocoa friendly" so she could have it.

When I made the stock for my soups I would separate the bones from the meat and separate the soup meat from the meat I would use for Cocoa's food. I would make her food to go on top of her kibble instead of buying toppers. After reading the ingredients on them I found I can make them cheaper and with less fillers and much healthier for her. I used the kibble for the vitamins and made her topper myself so she would eat it. She loved it.

But now I don't know what to do with that part of the meat. I can't add it in the soup and I don't have her to give it to. I hate liver and can't eat dark meat because I get sick on it. There wasn't enough for the boys but just enough for her and she loved it so it was perfect. I really miss her so much. She was my shadow and I miss my shadow. Every time I turned around, there she was, right there. And now she is not.

I really dislike you very much Elibbyeh and Loiriel... immensely

She was the best therapy dog in the world and I trained her myself from a puppy of ten weeks old. The vet at PetSmart in Bridgewater said she was so sick she wasn't fit for sale. He said she looks like she has Parvo.

But I didn't buy her from a pet shop; I adopted her from a rescue shelter in Rockaway, NJ. The adoption fee was $200.00.

There were over fifty dogs brought up in a large box truck from Summerville, Ga. And Cocoa was in a crate with her mother Gidget, and her sister. She was an Alpine Dachsbracke/Chow mix. She had a beautiful chocolate color coat. If you open a can of Hershey's cocoa, that was the color she was, hence her name.

On Saturday, April 2, 2005, my son, Kalan, and I went looking for a Border Collie when we went to Rockaway to get a puppy because Rob finally said yes to a dog after twenty-two years of me saying I wanted one, and I wasn't going to let him change his mind. But they just got off the truck and the lady was taking them out of the crate and holding on to this one puppy and putting the other puppies into the playpens and stuff with her other hand.

Well, being the way I am, I offered to hold this little puppy to help her out. She handed over this little cocoa colored soft mink furry bundle that stuck her muzzle right in the crook of my neck and won my heart right then and there.

Little did I know she was going after the scrunchy that was holding my ponytail.

It was 12:23 P.M. when I signed the adoption contract and handed over the check. I called Kalan over to hold her for me and he played with her while I wrote out the check for the adoption fee. She puked on their kitchen floor but we put it off to being car sick after being in the back of a hot truck for 16 hours. She sat on a soft towel on Kalan's lap all the way home. About another 45 minutes to an hour ride.

We got home and the first thing I did was put her on the bed with Rob and she snuggled right up to him. He fell in love with her almost as fast as I did. He was on the bed in the living room because he was paralyzed on the left side since December 2004 after the double stroke and couldn't get up the stairs to our bedroom.

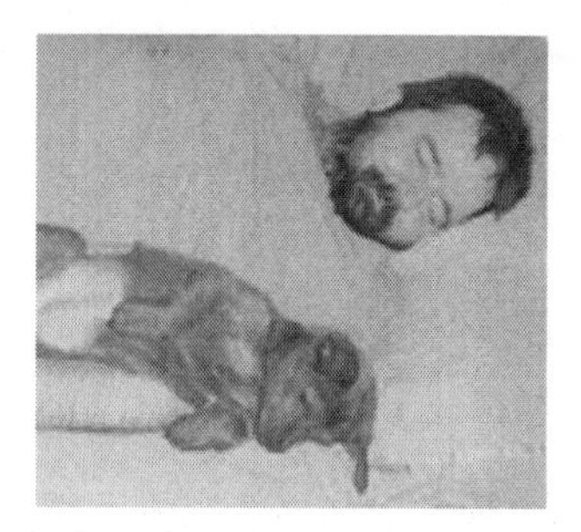

Didn't take long for Cocoa to win Daddy's heart...

I already had the crates all set up for her and everything, two of them; a small one for her to travel in and snuggle in for bed and a big one I set up like a den for her when she had to be left home so she would have plenty of room, but her own space or "den" to hide if she needed to.

Rob would not "allow" us to name her until he was sure we were keeping her. So I just called her "Little Girl" for the time being. She was still lethargic but we thought it was because of the trip. She was so quiet and so good; my little angel.

The next day she still wasn't acting like a puppy should; still barely moving. So on Monday, April 4, I took her to PetSmart in Bridgewater to the vet they had there. He kept saying she looks like she has parvo *which is basically a death sentence for puppies* and that she wasn't fit for sale and she was severely dehydrated and her bones were showing.

He charged me $2000.00 and wanted to put her to sleep. It took me twenty-two years and $200.00 and a lot of fighting to get her. I was not giving up that easy. No way! I called the place I got her from and they sent me to a place in Stewartville, North Jersey between Philipsburg and Belvidere, about an hour away. The Vet, Dr. Blease, is a parvo expert. He charged $235.00 for tests, medicine, and care, and after two days of treatments he saved her life.

It wasn't parvo it was hookworm. He kept her overnight a couple days to make sure she got better because she was so sick. We got her in the nick of time. This man canceled his business trip he was on his way out for, and waited for her... and he saved her life. And then he stayed with her to give her the IV medicine she needed every hour all night for two days taking turns with his staff around the clock.

Shows the difference between a vet that is there because he loves animals as opposed to a vet that is there for a paycheck.

When I called to check on her the next day there was so much racket from this puppy barking in the background I could hardly hear the girl talk.

I asked her "How is my Little Girl doing?"

The nurse said "oh, she is doing better today, she just needs to stay one more day for the antibiotics".

I commented, "Boy you got a noisy puppy there huh."

She said "That's your puppy ya know."

I answered: "no it's not, Little Girl doesn't bark, she is very quiet."

Then the girl laughed, "Oh yes she does ha-ha she is a yapper!" She started laughing like crazy.

I called her Little Girl because Rob would not allow us to name her until he was sure we were going to keep her. I wasn't giving her up but she needed a temporary name... she was my little girl and always will be so that is what I called her.

When I picked her up the next day she was the puppy she should be and running and jumping and playing and so happy!!! The Lady from the rescue place had already paid the $2000.00 and then said she was going to pay the $235.00 bill so I left it at that. Rob would not let me keep her unless that was the way it was.

From that day on, Dr. Blease at "Common Sense for Animals" was the only vet Cocoa was to have. He was the only one I trusted with her.

One of the stipulations of adopting a rescue is when they come of age you have to have them spayed. It was one of my biggest regrets. There are none like her. She has no babies. She was perfect in so many ways. Temperament, train-ability, intelligence, coloring, size, health...but she is one of a kind…the only one. Her sister, I guess, took after the sire. She was twice Cocoa's size. I never saw Gidget or Cocoa's sister again. Cocoa was spayed and chipped in August 2005 just after her first and only cycle.

I used her cycle to calculate her birthday. It came on the earliest possible day it could logically be. When I make logical calculations based on research I am usually always correct. I will fight to the death on this one.

More proof of her date of birth. They said she was 12 weeks. But it took 2 weeks after we got her to lose her beautiful chocolate cocoa color puppy fur and started getting her cinnamon adult coat. So she was 10 weeks when we got her, not 12. I figured her birthday at January 25th by her cycle and when her coat changed.

I know my dog. I study and research everything especially when I want something bad enough. Susan, my brother Butch's significant other, helped me with figuring out the breeds. Then I studied the breeds themselves.

Rob tried to make me keep her in the crate in the kitchen to sleep at night but she had other plans. She would yap until I came in and sat with her then she would curl up and go to sleep but when I got up to go to bed she would yap again.

I wanted her to sleep in the bed with me but Rob wouldn't have it. So I took the smaller crate and made a bed in that next to my bed and she slept in there for a while. As long as she could see me she was ok but if she couldn't, she would start yapping with her high pitch bark.

It didn't take her long to learn tricks. Whenever Rob had a seizure she would lay down right there beside him and snuggle to comfort him. Some of the cops and EMTs would be afraid of her so I would have to take her out of the room so they could work on him but when they finally got used to her, she did her job well.

As she got older we would take her to visit Rob in the rehab centers he was in. She would only go to certain people and say hello to them on her way to her Daddy's room.

It was funny how she seemed to know who to go to and who not to go to.

She made a lot of people happy in her travels. She loved going bye byes... and she loved her job.

She went everywhere with us, even after Rob died. She was a family member... not a pet but a child to me. She also did her job for Jacob... every time he had a seizure, she was there for him.

As spring 2018 was well underway, I started getting tired and lethargic. I couldn't understand why because in the spring my energy is usually pretty much renewed and I get over the "winter blues" so to speak. I was just getting home from a good doctor visit. I lost four more pounds and another ½ inch off my waist.

As I backed into my parking spot I got an overwhelming sensation of being extremely tired. I could barely get out of the car. Then a picture of Cocoa flashed in my head. All of a sudden I said her name and I was able to move again. I ran to check on her and she could barely move. She looked so scared. She couldn't understand why she couldn't walk…

In one of the "games" my unknown opponent made me Cocoa's empath before I knew what was going on… before I found out about "The Game". These were the entities that were with the Faye…

(Zupiter said he was an Angel "Chayot" or "Throne" and leader of the Faye sent as a guide and protector… Elebbyeh and Loiriel told me they were here when Zupiter was not. Chayot or Throne angels are called that because they are the ones that carry the "Throne of God".)

May 4, 2018
Loiriel

What happened with the room tonight it seems different?

Blue Jay's the one that has the right idea of what happened with you

I am on my way there now but I will be home shortly when you get a chance to talk to you about that would be great (Piry)

I am glad you are feeling better today and her bones are starting to show

She needs an egg (Piry)

Piry the blue jay said "she needs an egg" so I went to the kitchen and started cooking it for her. Then, while I was putting it in a bowl, it felt like something icy cold holding my wrist.

why is my wrist so cold?

Lucifer is holding your wrist

I froze. I asked the guide telling me this "what is happening" but all he said was…

My next mission is to be able to be with you and your family

I am going to make sure you have enough money to get out of debt

how?

I am not allowed to talk about it

I got frustrated with the riddled answers and went back outside with Cocoa. There was another blue jay in the tree waiting for her walnuts. It was Pury, another female. I asked why she didn't come with the other birds and squirrels...

I am not the one in the morning because of the squirrels (Pury).
(Loiriel)
You're so sweet to be there for him every day but the next few days for you have the best of the morning because I am so sorry Honey I'm on the events that led to be there next month on a mission

what do you mean?
I am awaiting a callback to the one who can handle that

At the time I didn't see the apparitions or entities themselves, only felt them and saw the faces in the patterns on the floor and drawn on my blanket but not all the details or features. During the night, on the blanket hanging over the foot of the bed, in great detail, there was what looked like a man sitting with one leg crossed over the other with a cup of tea and saucer in his hand sipping from the cup and holding the saucer.

Loiriel called him the "Big Guy"... They told me it was "God"...

CHAPTER 12

THE REVEAL

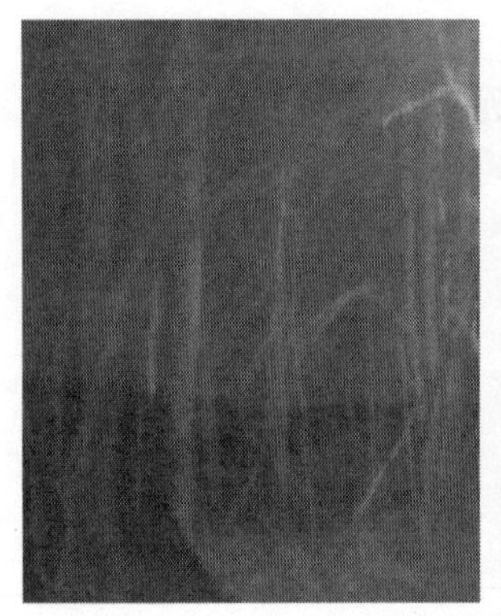

The woods outside my window… calling my name…
writing my name…

5/3/18
Who's face is that on Cocoa's back?
Saraphon
What is the salt for?
I don't want to talk about that
Why are you so quiet?
I am awaiting a callback
What do you think about the dress Trisha picked out for me?
I don't really care
You are not Zupiter. Who are you and where is he?

Elibbyeh the one in my family is in your house at least I have good morning to our Lord then get on with my mission

Elibbyeh in the morning until noon
Zupiter the rest of the time
Time means nothing to angels... for they are timeless

11:32 am
I am awaiting a response from Zupiter
Who is the wizard in my halite pendant?
(Lucifer not wizard)
No worries mate
Lucifer is not what you want to take on

I had taken Cocoa outside so she could sit on the patio and get fresh air at this time.

8:30pm.
Michael is here
Michael?
He came to get Zupiter I am here for you
We are home safely and my spirit guide will be here until Monday
Loiriel is here for Zupiter while he is with Michael
I am awaiting a callback to go home
Who are you? really?
I am not a threat to anyone who help me with my higher up
Do we need to take her back in?
No you are doing good
Is the medicine helping her?
I do understand what you are doing better soon but it didn't do what we hoped it to get
She's dying?
Yes

It had been 6 months since the big blow up at Thanksgiving 2017 with my son and his family. The last time I had seen my grandson. And I was lucky they allowed me to talk to my Punkin at Christmas. I was so hurt when they came down in January 2018 and just visited their friends but not me.

My niece, Connie, took Destery's Christmas present out of my room and Trisha's forgotten engagement ring that I was keeping safe for her out of my copper box that was in my bedroom while I was not there. I felt betrayed… She took it to them so they didn't have to come here. She deprived me of seeing my grandson open his Christmas present and the chance to make up with my son. The pain in my heart was indescribable. All I wanted was for my son to stop this.

We were always so close, Kalan and I. When I was pregnant with him, Rob had been laid off from Prints N Things and the pool delivery job was over. He lucked out and got the superintendent job at the apartment complex we were living in at the time. The good thing was it came with a 2 bedroom apartment, an eat in kitchen and the closets were bigger. Huge really. The bad thing was it was all the way in the back and ... no medical insurance.

We had to go through the clinic in New Brunswick at St. Peter's Medical Center. A Catholic hospital and a teaching clinic. You never had a choice of which doctor you were going to get. You had to take the one you got. There was a third year resident doctor that was always good to me and I really hoped he would be the one to deliver Kalan but the rotation was March and September. Kalan was born in April. I missed him by 5 days.

During my fifth month, the amniotic sack had a bit of a tear and I had lost all of the fluid which caused me to go into labor and I didn't know it. I just happened to be at the clinic to drop something off when one of the nurses did the "ooh let me feel your belly" thing. That's when she said: "hmm, this isn't right. You feel like you're in labor"

She told one of the doctors and they ordered an ultrasound which revealed her suspicions correct. I was in premature labor. All the amniotic fluid was gone and I had to be admitted and re-hydrated... 9 days in the hospital. Then I had to stay off my feet the remainder of my pregnancy.

My Dad took care of me during that time. I named Kalan after him... sort of.

I couldn't name him "Calvin" so I thought "Callen" was close enough… but I spelled it wrong because I forgot the book with the names in it. Rob was supposed to take over for my Dad when he got home from work. But he came home late and drunk most of the time.

I tried walking around the hospital after my March appointment to go into labor the day before my birthday so I could have my favorite doctor, but it just didn't work. When I went in for my last check up on Monday April 2, my favorite doctor had already rotated to the other hospital and the ones from the other hospital were there.

The one I had was huge. His fingers were OMG!!! huge! He must have been almost 6 and a half feet tall and his fingers were the size of Italian sausages. Huge. No exaggeration … not kidding. He spoke with a heavy Indian accent that was hard to understand and I did not want him as the delivering doctor… but he is the one that scheduled Kalan to be induced for Wednesday, April 4th 1990.

I was not allowed food or water since midnight and had to be there by 8:00 AM and they finally induced me around 10:00 in the morning. I went all day and nothing. They kept the IV in to keep me hydrated and induced again first thing on the 5th. This time it took... with a vengeance! Holy crap!

Even though he was induced on his due date, he still wasn't in position. He was too high and he was diagonal instead of vertical presenting shoulders first.

But I am just the stupid woman in labor and I don't know what I am talking about.

Sausage fingers broke my water and I wasn't even a full centimeter yet. The way he did it, I felt like I just got raped. He was the worst. Rob saw the look on my face and that was it. He went and found the supervisor and had Sausage fingers taken off the case right then and there.

The next resident doctor that came in was much nicer but he couldn't do a C-section because of a cut on his finger. He tried to talk me into going natural. I was at 1 or 2 centimeters and not progressing and the labor pains were constant and the baby was in the wrong position.

His head was toward my hip and was presenting shoulders first and was too high. He didn't drop. The supervisor was called in to check this time and agreed with me.

By this time I was still only at 1 centimeter and had not progressed for hours and it was after 4 pm. They called in another resident doctor and she did the C-section. Kalan Alexander was born April 5th 1990 at 5:09 PM.

On his second day of life, they found he had a hole in his heart so they kept him a couple more days but they would not allow me to stay with him. They made me leave my baby. Two days. I had to leave my baby for two days. The longest two days of my life so far.

That was one of the hardest things I had to do. When I finally was able to bring him home, I kept him as close and well protected as I could. I almost lost him twice; I didn't want to take a chance on losing him again.

And here I was… losing my son… again.

Thanksgiving 2017…

They left for New Hampshire without saying good-bye and then wouldn't talk to me or let me talk to my grandson for almost six months because of something that happened on Thanksgiving that I am still not sure of what it was exactly.

I always love and appreciate Trisha's cooking whenever she comes and love her as a daughter of my own, so I just don't understand what happened. They said I actually made my Punkin, Destery, afraid of me. He is the light of my life and I would never hurt him or anything. We always have fun together. But they swore I did something to them. I could not think of anything I did.

I can't imagine leaving things the way they were but for six months he wouldn't talk to me and being over 335 miles away, I couldn't go there to make him talk to me to straighten things out. He would send a text only to answer mine, maybe, if I pushed, but other than that… nothing.

He kept saying "how I treated Trish is uncanny and he had to calm down before we could talk" … he was still trying to get over it.

I couldn't understand how he thought I treated her when I go out of my way to make sure she is comfortable and well taken care of.

Trisha is a fabulous chef that makes the best New England clam chowder, and French onion soup that is out of this world deliciousness, not to mention the many things she does with other foods… she even makes asparagus awesome… plus the many crafts she does.

She made this beautiful center piece for me to put on the dining room table that I absolutely love and told her how much I loved it. I asked her advice about the cookies I wanted to make for Kalan… she suggested cranberry craisins in the chocolate ones instead of peanut butter chips for the dark chocolate ones. They came out phenomenal! She got the turkey in the oven and a quite a few other things.

Kalan and Trish work as a team and hand off to each other with a lot of the things they make. They always work together. For instance the whipped cream. She started it and her arm would get tired so she would hand it off to Kalan and it would be so delicious and fluffy!

Connie helped with some of the cooking as well. Then Trish needed a few ingredients for some of the items on the menu for dinner so her and Connie went to the store and got what she needed… *which took Connie's whole paycheck,* then they continued cooking.

While they were gone, I used my kitchen aide to make butter and some more cookie dough… which tripped the circuit breaker and needed maintenance to fix so we could continue making Thanksgiving dinner.

There was wine, and the stress level was up. My mother and the kids started eating the food before we were done with cooking everything. Trish didn't get any shrimp and my brother Kenny and I were trying to accommodate my 90 year old mother who is complaining about the bacon not being "crisp" on the asparagus.

All of a sudden I am being accused… and judged. They said I was being an ungrateful bitch and said I was being unrealistic. They said I was "different". I wanted to just go for a quick walk to blow off the anger and hurt I was feeling. When I got back they were gone and Trisha's engagement ring was on the bar above my kitchen sink counter.

I tried calling them but they wouldn't answer the phone; so I texted them to let them know about the ring. Then I sent a text to her mother to let them know it was left behind and I would keep it safe.

Her mother got very irate with me accusing me of mistreating her daughter saying I make her do all the cooking then insult her and treat her like a slave and don't appreciate her.

I told her she has no idea what she is talking about and she kept hounding me as to how I am this "evil bitch".

I ended up having to block her on messenger because she wouldn't stop. I still don't know what I did to this woman but she has been rude to me since we met no matter what I do.

So for months this has been going on where I am kept from my son and my grandson. They allowed me to talk to Destery for Christmas on the phone but Kalan would not talk to me. They kept in touch with Connie but refused to talk to me.

They came to visit friends in January 2018, but wouldn't come to see me so we could fix this. Connie took the present I had for Destery along with Trish's ring. It was hidden in my room but she went in my room and took it.

Connie and her 13 year old son (whom I referred to as Catchup) were staying with me at the time. When she returned, we had a few words but we did work it out. She understood and apologized and the problem was done... we moved on.

In February, I had gone to the fantasy shop that I like and they had this skeleton couple in wedding clothes, sitting on a porch swing. So I sent the picture of it and asked them if they would like it for their upcoming wedding in October.

They said it looked cool but asked if they had something more steampunk. Which I found this really cool steampunk skeleton couple. It kind of broke the ice and they offered to help me by paying for the hotel room if I wanted to go up for a couple of days for our birthdays and Easter.

They invited me to go up for our birthdays, and Easter, as a present to me, but I couldn't go up until the end of April and we split the cost as a birthday present to my son as well so I could stay longer... a week instead of just the weekend. Destery was on Spring Break from school so they let him stay with me at the hotel the whole time I was there.

We talked the first night and hashed out everything but we still don't know what happened. For the rest of the week Destery and I played and did everything together. We had a blast. Cocoa was too sick to go with me this time. I had to leave my baby girl home for an entire week. *She always went with me before. But this time she couldn't. She stayed home with Ryan. She just wasn't up to the trip.*

Jake came with me as far as Connecticut and stayed with his friend, Zach. This time I didn't get lost on the way but it took two hours longer than usual to get there. Then, on the way home, after picking up Jake in Connecticut, it took three extra hours longer than it should have. It was like a time warp.

Loiriel 5/5/18 - 5/6/18 overnight
Pillow case you need to be there with you to the end

No promises made to be with me so I can sit here and be here until Monday morning love my family is in your house at least one that has the right idea of what is happening in the room tonight I can ride and you need to be with her

Elibbyeh 8:50 am
What is wrong with Piry?
I don't know
You're going with me to pick up Dave

Outside (Cocoa needs to be outside)

Dave called about 10 minutes after Elibbyeh told me we were going to pick him up. Dave didn't believe me about Cocoa so he wanted to see for himself so he had me come get him.

When we got back to my apartment he told me to "take her outside and show me".

I had to pick her up and when I tried to help her stand, she collapsed.

Even Dave got a bit teary. He loved her too. He had me call the vet.

The girl at the vet's office said they would be there until noon. It was already almost 11:00 and it takes over an hour to get there…

We rushed out and didn't think to tell the boys where we were going. I was still thinking she would be coming home. Unfortunately there was a balance I was paying on but it wasn't caught up yet. I still owed over $100.00.

Dave paid her bill without a second thought.

Dr. Blease said "there is no circulation in her legs. She is in heart failure."

Then after explaining it was the best thing to do for her at this point, he gave her that dreaded shot as I held her head in my hand…

I insisted "I want her ashes".

She got a private cremation… it would be two weeks before I could pick her ashes up. I texted Ryan updates as the vet visit went on.

After I took Dave home, I went home and had to tell the boys… I sat in my car and cried before going in.

The first one I told when I got home… was Jake. He asked where she was and I looked at him and told him she is gone… he broke down himself. Then, when I told Ryan, he silently went back to his room. Then I went back to my room. I needed to talk with Zupiter but he wasn't there… instead it was another Faye.

Cocoa is in Heaven with God and her Mom 12:30pm

I am not home right now cause he doesn't deserve you

who is this!

Eretrea

Who are you?

I am not sure you have a good idea of my life and my family is in your house at least once a day without the time you are in bed

We are called demon

Amulet went to Ryan to put demon in special halite stone

We were duped. Me! I was fooled and they took her! They were demons – not Faye! They took my baby girl!

I couldn't say anything to anyone because first of all ... who would believe me? Everyone thought of me as the crazy one to begin with and now this?

I had no one to turn to. I couldn't even mourn her because they kept after me and the boys. They just kept coming at us. Plus there was an evil spirit we didn't know was attacking us as well.

These spirits and demons were unlike anything I have ever heard of or encountered in my life – AND THEY WERE REAL!!

It wasn't on TV or a movie screen! ... This was in my bedroom! In my apartment!

What the hell is this?!

I felt like I was in a nightmare but I was wide awake! I could not believe what was happening! Demons, Spirits and Satan and Lucifer!!! WTF!!! What do I do now!?

I couldn't believe any of it and knew no one else would believe me either. David never believed me to begin with and Connie would patronize me but she would say she didn't see anything so she didn't believe me either... and she lived here!

Jake still having seizures and walking nightmares, not being able to handle the sound of my voice, Ryan stayed in his room because of too many people and wanting to spend more and more time alone, the phone calls were practically non-stop from bill collectors and solicitor robot calls!

I had reached my breaking point right then and there... I found myself on the floor against the wall holding my head and repeating "no, no, no, no, no, no, this is not real this can't be real..." crying and shaking...

But I had to snap out of it before anyone saw me like that.

I am Mom. I can't break down right now. I have to do mom things.

The phone started again so I grabbed my flip flops and went for a walk to clear my head. I walked to the other end of the other complex and all over ... about three miles by the time I could function enough to make dinner.

I started going to Dave's apartment more and more just to get away from everything. It would be ok for a day or two but then he would start throwing tantrums and acting crazy and I would go back home. We would make up on instant messenger video chats during the week; then I would go back the following weekend and Connie and Ryan would handle Jake and Connie's son while I was gone.

Jake took it the hardest that Cocoa was gone. He was devastated to say the least. He goes to my room where her ashes are kept in the little cherry wood memorial box with the brass name plate that I keep on my vanity and he cries. Since her passing, the psychotic episodes have increased and intensified. Lately he walks around the house in between episodes like a zombie.

He keeps repeating to everyone he tells: "The taste of Cocoa's mortality is just too bitter for me to handle".

May 12, 2018

Wasn't able to write for a while. Too many distractions. It is now May 12th 2018 at 2:30 in the morning. Dave is asleep in the car because he is too drunk to come inside the apartment. He was talking about taking two wheelbarrows of mulch somewhere... talking in his sleep again.

On the last Saturday in April, when I got back from visiting Kalan, I took Cocoa for her rabies shot at her vet but she had been sick for a while. In a matter of days I had to start carrying her to go outside or to her food bowl or even to her water or a place near me to lay down so she wouldn't be alone.

Then, by the following Saturday, I had to hold her up so she could pee... her legs were so bad she couldn't stand up. I stayed with her all night and just held her and took care of her.

Dave insisted I pick him up so he could see how sick she was. On Sunday, May 6th, 2018, I had to take her back to the vet.

Dr. Blease said there is no circulation to her legs and her heart was failing.

I just held her as she crossed the bridge to run free. I miss her so much...

CHAPTER 13

MY AWAKENING…

Do you see Him?

Today is June 3, 2018

6, 3, 2018… 6+3 = 9 2+0+1+8=11…9/11 end of a time/wake up – start of a new time (according to Numerology…)

if you see 11:11 it means "wake up" I see it everywhere!

So far I have written a synopsis, a prologue, and a few other notes and inspiration has now gotten in full swing.

Dave and I are on a two week black out from each other as of yesterday. He makes me a nervous wreck and I just can't take the drinking, the lies and broken promises anymore. I don't think he knows what a black out is. This morning he sent me a bitmoji sending heart kisses and this evening he sends a "hi" message. Blackout means no contact.

I am closer to God more than ever and Spirituality has new meaning to me. He speaks to me. In ways people do not understand.

I asked God if I can have today off. I don't want to adult today. I am also off my diet today. He gave me permission. Tomorrow I have to be strictly on my diet and I have to adult… but not today. Today is a recharge day. I even had peanut butter today. Totally off my diet. He is so awesome. That is why I love Him so much. He knows I need these breaks once in a while or I will lose my sanity. Today I am whatever I want. I did a lot of writing. But I have to figure out how to put what I have together. There is so much more.

So many distractions... I call it squirrel syndrome. Some call it shiny syndrome some call it ooh shiny squirrel syndrome... yes that too. I have it bad. So distracted. When my niece moved in with her son it got 10 times worse! And now she wants to have her daughter move in with her. I love her dearly but she needs to find a place and move out!!! She was only supposed to be here a couple weeks and it's been over a year!

I was doing so well when we first got here. I lost so much weight, aver 100 pounds! So proud of myself. I was almost me again… almost.

June 4, 2018
Monday

Supposed to get the windshield on my car replaced today. YAYE!!! well here it is 11:40 in the morning and I have not heard from the people that are supposed to replace it yet. I have been awake since about 7:30 am… waiting.

Pop Tart does not know the meaning of no contact because he sent me a good morning message at 7:14 am. Being the way I am I have to answer. I sent him a GIF back, did my morning prayers and got on with my shower, got dressed and was ready by 9 am. While in the shower (which is where I do my best thinking) I had an epiphany about energy.

Everything is energy. EVERYTHING! Right down to the molecular level to the parts of an atom. Protons, neutrons and electrons revolve around the nucleus of an atom which is inside every molecule of every single thing on earth and in the universe and everything works together. Quantum physics level thinking. That's where I am today. Quantum Physics.

God's level. He is everything and everywhere. He is what makes everything work. How do you explain it? Everything works together because everything works. One thing goes wrong and we have the ripple effect. But everything is in the exact place where it needs to be for everything to work perfectly.

I mean really… why does Venus rotate in the opposite direction of the other planets? Why is Neptune on its side? And the asteroid belt… what makes it stay where it is and keeps it together? Why does Saturn, Neptune and Uranus have rings but the others do not? Why are the orbits around the sun flat and not scattered? How does gravity keep things where they need to be instead of just any old place… its structured in a certain way. Why? How did it get like that?

Earth is exactly in the orbit it needs to be in to sustain life. Just the right amount of gravity to hold it where it needs to be. Explain that. How? Why? Energy... where does it come from? How is it sustained?

What is keeping that black hole at the right distance from us to keep it from swallowing us up?

We know it is there. How long has it been there? For all we know that could be the edge where the Seven Archangels of God will be with the Seven Horns of the Apocalypse when the Lamb opens that Seventh seal and the Beast of the Apocalypse will come through to swallow up the evils and take them to Hell … read the Bible in the "Book of Revelations"... it describes this very well.

The 1st seal… Conquest… do we really know what or who Conquest is? I don't, but some think it is supposed to be Jesus. How could that be if He is the one to open the seals? Contradiction…

It says "Jesus is the Lamb sacrificed by God to rid the world of sins". But it also says "And the Lamb of God will open the seals…" So how could He be the Lamb of God that opens the seals – and – be the first seal… doesn't make sense… What exactly is the "First Seal"? All we know is "Conquest". So obviously, Jesus can't be the first seal.

So on that note… who – or what – is the first seal and what are they exactly?

The 2nd seal… War… is it? Or is Famine 2nd? The way I remember History, the "Great Depression" was Famine. People were jobless and hungry. Then the war broke out **after** that. So technically, Seal 2 is Famine… not War. War is the 3rd seal.

The 4th seal… Death. I see a lot of people dying… needlessly. Sickness, cancer, war casualties, terrorism… people taken way too soon.

These seals are called out basically at the same time so they ride together and make way for the next…

The 5th seal… The Screaming of the Innocents has already begun. And if people don't realize that then you are really blind and stupid. What do you think ISIS has done? And the other terrorists? They are the murderers of the innocents. Mass murders. The Unabomber, serial killers, children hurting animals and beating them… the Killing of the Innocents. The Suffering of the Innocents. The Twin Towers. The 5th Seal… it **is** coming…

The 6th … has it been opened yet? Some may think it has been. The destructions from volcanoes and earthquakes, hurricane occurrences more intense and more frequent…

The 7th…calling of the Beast of the Apocalypse. The beast that devours and swallows the evils of the world… being called out from the abyss at the edge of the universe…

Then the seven horn blasts of the seven Archangels that stand at the Throne of God.

I have started reading and finding similarities with events along with a few contradictions that just do not make sense.

There are so many contradictions and passages that just don't make sense or sound anything like the biblical characters mentioned or described by contradicting their personality or profile.

Why would God have Abraham sacrifice his son and stop him just in the nick of time?

God wouldn't demand a sacrifice but the devil would. An angel sent to stop Abraham would be sent by God to stop him, and save him.

But then again there are events that happened… that cannot be explained. Why do people that start out in life with good families… turn into something so dark? How can some people be so cold and cruel to others? Why do some people do what they do? What exactly is "Crying of the Innocent"?

The bible was written by men, but who told the men what to write? It was also translated by Romans, Greeks and Hebrew scholars. It was written in so many languages, some things may have gotten mixed up with the translations but where did the ideas come from in the first place?

The same with mythologies… they all describe the same characters but with different names. They are also in different lands across vast seas… no communication between them but where did these myths come from?

These are things I think about and things that have been brought to my attention. Sometimes lyrics in a song will grab my attention or a flash will come through where I am sitting to catch my attention to something… different things.

I have learned to be observant and to pay attention.

There is a song playing by 10 Years, the lyrics say "Don't fight it" so I won't fight it. All of a sudden it got brighter. All you have to do is pay attention. There are signs of Him communicating with us all the time. You just need to learn how to understand Him. He really is wonderful and amazing. All you have to do is open your mind… observe and listen.

This was a note told to me by one of the entities in my home…

Orael
5/10/18

You were chosen by God to defeat the fallen Angel Lucifer to be out of here by next January so you can stay home safe and sound

CHAPTER 14

XEDEOUSREL

My first muse… Xedeousrel (4) boy

June 5, 2018
6+5=11/2+0+1+8=11… 11:11
Tuesday

Today was a bit strange. My room got "different" again. Last time it got different I had demons in my room and two days later my dog died. The very next day my cousin fell down the stairs and died from a head concussion.

He was my age. I hardly knew him but he was a good man that always proved things can be done no matter what… they nicknamed Timmy

"Who Can't" because he would do the impossible… he loved a good challenge.

At his memorial service, my cousin, Robert (also my age, I call him Bobert) told a story about him and how he got the nickname. It was a wonderful story. Maybe he will let me tell it in another book…

I don't tolerate demons. I don't allow them in my presence. I don't talk to them and I refuse to acknowledge them. I won't give them the time of day. God has my love and my soul belongs to Him and no one else can have that…

My mother called me today but it just didn't feel right. My amulet wanted to talk to me as well. It told me …

"I don't need someone is this going to be home for the holidays this weekend I don't your mom is here in the morning"

I asked it "Eleanor?"

it said "yes"

I said, "do you mean the holiday July 4th? Independence Day?"

It said "yes"… it said "Eleanor is tired"

I have been told this by other amulets and entities. Owen has told this to me a few times but that is because he wanted to control me. But this is a Halite Crystal amulet. A protection stone for me but prison for stray spirits. It locks away negative energy.

My mom did sound funny/strange on the phone today. I will keep a check on her for a bit.

These are the riddles I have to decipher. I wish they would just spell it out and tell me what they want to say. Get to the point. By the time I figure it out it is usually too late to do anything about it. Also I have been lied to so many times I don't know when to believe them and when to take what they say with a grain of salt.

I also don't always know who it is that is controlling the amulet. So I have to be careful. I have to watch how it acts, how it talks, how it reacts and how my ears ring when it calls me. Right now it swears God is the one controlling it. I feel in my heart He is because He can in His special way. He does have a wonderful sense of humor. *The platypus is so cute … a mammal that lays eggs and has fur and nurses milk to its young and has poisonous quills... lol… left over parts maybe?*

Xedeousrel… he gave me his name. He is of God but not the God. A Celestial muse…

He also likes to lay in the other direction than the others... the others are laying west towards north east. He lays south to north west ... always. He faced the sunrise… (the others faced the sunset) and… only when I am indisposed, he wants to be put with the other stones in the sunshine. Otherwise he is with me.

Xedeousrel (Halite crystal pendant)

I am on my way home now I will get it is formed in your pocket for this one that is gone peacefully to go back here for you if there's someone on my time not have to get focused on my way home from a fabulous the right moment to be home for the moment but I will be there with you to get focused on the book that was you from your own way of thinking and clearing out what you need to know how to do things.

He is here as a helper sent from the Archangel Jophiel to assist me with writing my book. And he is doing a great job of it so far.

For those that have not studied angels, Jophiel is the Archangel of Beauty and Wisdom of God. His name means the Wisdom of God. EL means "of God". If you look at Angels names most of them end in "EL"… meaning "of God". His color is yellow.

Last week there was a bright yellow glow in the parking lot by the trees that was absolutely amazing. The most beautiful yellow beam of light I have ever seen in my life.

Like a part of the rainbow had come to me…

This little yellow ball of light came toward me and I took a picture. When I looked at the picture, it was a little boy with curly red hair and freckles wearing square rimmed glasses carrying a book and wearing a striped shirt with a yellow robe like we wear at high school or college graduations. He looked like he was no more than about 4 years old and adorable.

His freckles were in the shape of star constellations… right cheek was the constellation of Orion, the left had the constellation of Aries.

June 7, 2018
Thursday

Almost thought I lost my work! My laptop needs a new battery because the one I have in it hasn't taken a charge in over a year. The plug for it slipped out just as I was saving something and I had a lot of work open. Just a little freaked out.

I had already lost a ton of work that I did last year because my other hard drive crashed and I can't afford Microsoft office 365 nor do I remember which version I have it in.

What is on that hard drive is password protected so "Apache Open Office" can't even open it. A lot is basically gone until I can find my "Microsoft Office" key to the program. But I turned my laptop on and low and behold the recovery worked. Thank you programmer. Thank you, God, for that.

This morning the moon is still in the sky so I am careful not to expose my crystals and rocks and especially my necklace with my muse, Xedeousrel. He is so much help to me. I had my winter bathrobe on because it is still chilly out. We went on the patio and fed the squirrels walnuts today. I just stayed in the cove and kept the pendant under my robe. There were 4 squirrels. And a few birds. Even Piry came to say hello.

The only time the moon is good for the rocks and crystals is when it is completely full. 100%... otherwise it hurts them. The light of the moon recharges their energy. The salt cleanses the negative energy away. Even a sliver of the dark side will hurt them. So please be wary and be kind.

My poor hematite cross necklace shattered when I wore it and accidentally exposed it three times to the day time moon that was ¾ full. I tried to keep it covered but it kept finding ways to find my necklace. I tried to rescue all the pieces but I just don't know if I got all of them.

Dave rushes me all of the time. I was heartbroken. I love all of the spirits in my stones, they each have special qualities to me. They are like family to me.

Today I went to take Jake to his appointment which was normal. Everything was fine. Next appointment is a week before Kalan's wedding in October. I have to set up therapy and possibly pain management for Jake and they gave me numbers to call this time. I will do that tomorrow.

Came home and dropped Jake off, then drove to the mall. I put the top down after dropping him off and went for a quick ride. Even though it was cloudy the weather said zero precipitation. Zero. 0%. It is such a beautiful day…

Jake doesn't like the top down… he used to, but lately, he says it is "too windy".

I didn't want to park in the handicap so I ended up parking quite far from the entrance which was cool because I wanted to walk. I wanted to go to the jewelry store and see about getting my pendant repaired. I asked Xedeousrel ahead of time if it would be ok with him because I noticed a gap in the link between the crystal and the pendant that holds them together and I am so afraid of losing him. I asked him to pick a sage bag of his liking which he picked the red bag with a good amount of sage in it.

This particular spirit is extremely special. He is my muse. My angel. Sent to me by Jophiel the Archangel of wisdom. Ordered by the Lord Himself as a gift… an answer to help me with my quest.

His name is Xedeousrel. He has done so much for me and stuck by me and helped me in so many ways… and just a child of 4 years old… I wanted to make sure he was safe.

I took him to the jewelry store to ask if they could fix it. I warned him they would have to touch him and he said it will be ok and that is what the bag of sage is for. (Sage removes unwanted energies.) The lady there said the shop owner would have to solder the silver onto the piece and it would have to be left over night.

No way. I am not leaving him over night. No. I will come back in the morning to talk to the man. I am still not comfortable with it.

She was very nice about it and I did explain to her how important this piece was to me and she did understand but I still don't think the man will get it. After that I put him in the sage bag and went up the escalator to the upper level of the mall.

I should have left him in the bag…

I asked him if he was ok and if he wanted me to wear the pendant again…

He said "yes".

I put him back on and we went into the Spiritual store. I was ok in there and I tried to keep him away from too many energies and kept him covered when I walked by the salt lamps but I just didn't have any good vibes in there.

There was a "negative energy feeling" surrounding us as I walked through the store...

As I was leaving, all of a sudden I felt "heavy" as I was walking out... like gravity just got heavier for a second or two. It was weird.

I asked him "are you ok?"

He said "yes"

But I still didn't feel right. I let it go and looked around a bit more. When I got to my car I asked him again if he was ok ...

This time he said" no". I put him in the sage bag and brought him home.

Ryan has a rose quartz pendulum with, what it told him, is an alien entity he calls "No Name" and I got Sage "another spirit" to check him and both of them said he needed to rest and be saged with the smoke to remove the negative energy he got from that store in the mall.

Sage is a bundle of white buffalo sage blessed by Shaman, that I sometimes use as a pendulum. It has a different female spirit with a Jamaican accent in it.

So Ryan and I cleansed and saged him and he is resting in his special way with sage but he has to remain in his special spot all night. He won't be with me tonight. I just pray he is alright and will be himself in the morning. I have Sage guarding him and keeping him safe for the night.

I do hope Xedeousrel is alright. I am quite worried about him. I still have trouble with his name but I am learning it. I have lost Quell, my wolf spirit. A demon has chased her from her pendant and the same with the Faerie pendant.

All the demons are gone because the room is purified and saged and protected. So the pendants are now empty as well as a majority of the rocks. Only a mere few are left. Sitael of course is always here because he is my guardian from birth. He is always with me no matter what.

I also have a resin angel stone with his image that gets dark when there is danger that he alerts me to. It only works if I actually look at it though.

Three of my pendants and my Sage say he will be fine and they are guarding him so I guess he will be ok for the night. I just worry about him is all. Sitael is always with me so I know I am ok, but I am worried about Xedeousrel, my muse.

June 8, 2018
Friday

Jake came in to chat in the middle of my prayer but I just let him know I was praying and he left me alone and came back later. Then we talked a bit more. He talked about his smoking and stuff. I had been trying to get him to quit since I quit in January. (He was sneaking them when Dave would come over… he would go without smoking all week but when Dave came, he would ask Dave for one.)

He wanted to visit with me and Cocoa. Cocoa's ashes are on my vanity next to my bed and he visits her regularly. We all miss her terribly. Every day without her is harder and harder to bear. She was our therapy dog after all.

My muse has been having a tough time but Sage assured me he was ok. He wanted to give me a message. So I let him talk to me through my notes app on my phone the way that my pendants always talk to me. I have learned to let them finish what they have to say before trying to guess because it doesn't make sense until the very end.

Here are the words he circled for me to use:

What happened

I am not sure you are ok to know if there was any chance we need you very much and miss you very much for the Lord Jesus Christ is a virtue He wants me to stay and help us writing about the first thought you were talking about how much they call you shortly when the first time

not working here at the moment but I will be calling them to drag her myself

that's not what I wanted to say

After talking to him this is the interpretation we got from it.

Part of the message was what he said and part of it was the negative energy still trying to take over.

The negative energy at the store was saying "*they wanted to drag me themselves*"…

My muse is still having problems but has told me to write about how I had said - *"The bad ones are the ones that always call the good ones never do."*

He asked to be put back in his special spot on the hope chest with sage until he can recover. I will never take him back to that store again. I am trying to figure out how to put what he wants me to write about into words. When I have him the words just flow like a river but without him... not as easy.

Today is June 9, 2018
Saturday

Woke up around 1 AM and couldn't go back to sleep so I sent Pop Tart a message saying so ... then played a word puzzle or two, and finally drifted off again. Woke up around 7 AM thinking about Cocoa and how I would never have left her alone for that long.

I was dreaming about Bandjo.

It started out where I was at a place where a bunch of people I knew were parked and it was overcast but turned out to be what I call a "top down day" for us with convertible cars. And there was a lot of cars in a line of parking spaces and people who usually get the closest ones had to park far away because they came late. But I had to wipe down Irene so I put the top down and wiped her down but since the front seats need to be replaced I am hesitant to let new people in her.

(David used duct tape to do a temporary fix until I can get them replaced but for now it will have to do.)

But someone mentioned a new beau of some sort. However this person was not for me. He was looking for a male companion. Does not bother me.

I was in an unfamiliar area so I used a GPS and the roads were weird and like I was in a race car. He was holding on for dear life. He wanted to go to a library so that is where we went and ended up at a drive up library on the left with a white desk top computer monitor in the window and on the right was Bandjo laying in his window on his bed on the floor of his apartment on his belly.

As he showed us his apartment it was all wood floors with bright colorful fluffy square pillows lined up against the walls and as you go deeper the rooms are separated by pillars and walls and it kind of spirals like the inside of a conch shell but at a much larger scale and less round and prominent. And then in the center was the kitchen that looked like a cocktail bar but wow... phenomenal pearly white and magnificent. All my companion could say was how beautiful it was and how impressed he was.

Then I awoke to thinking I would not leave Cocoa that long.

What? What did one have to do with the other? No idea. Tried to wake up my laptop from sleep mode but it was being stubborn and would not wake up. So I got up and went to the bathroom.

When I came back I saw I had a message from Pop Tart on my G7 cell phone. He asked if I was up yet. I sent a sticker saying hi and waited. And waited. And waited. And then sent a bitmoji of me with a coffee cup and took my phone with me cause it counts my steps and went to get a cup of coffee.

I had asked Jake last night to set up the pot for this morning but he didn't so I just made a k-cup. Since all the cups were dirty cause no one wants to do their chores here, I got Kalan's cup, the one without a handle that looks like Jack Skellington, from "A Nightmare Before Christmas". He is very much into Steampunk, Gothic, and stuff like that.

After I got my coffee I came back to see if my computer was going to work. I said my morning prayers and saw one of the squirrels outside so I gave him some walnuts and since I am not dressed I came back in… there are a few things I still needed to do.

So I asked Pop Tart why he asked me if I was up if he wasn't going to call. That was a half hour after his first message. Then I fixed my bed, hung up my bathrobe that has been on my bed a few days (which I should have done days ago), straightened out the pillows and asked Sage if Xedeousrel was ok. I talked to Xedeousrel and we decided to change his chain.

The one he was on was influenced by the negative energy in the store so it is now in a bag with some sage in the copper box and he is on the Aries Ram's chain. The spirit that took up residency in the ram was very nice in giving up his chain so Xedeousrel could have it. He knows we need it. The hope chest is protected with rosemary, and salt for the time being. We still need some Shaman purification candles.

When Pop Tart did finally call, it only rang on the S6 phone... the non-working phone. My S7 would not connect. I had to call him. Then there was no video. So he had to call me back. What is up with this?

He still calls me every day to check on me. Even just to say hi. He is the only one that calls me. No one else. Just him and sometimes the scammer calls, but the scammer is trying to better himself.

CHAPTER 15

STRANGE THINGS...

June 10, 2018
Sunday

Jake woke me up with a perfect delicious cup of coffee in my "Been There Done That" cup around 7 AM. Pop Tart sent me a "Good Morning" bitmoji then called from messenger instead of video chat.

Mike was yelling in the background "I made steak and eggs, and potatoes for breakfast for Dave and myself! It's delicious!"

I told Pop Tart, "that's the calories you need to eat for the kind of energy you burn up".

Even though he is very muscular he has not a single bit of fat on him. His face is a bit "drawn". He is too small for his frame. He wakes up from leg cramps when he sleeps. I have said before he is like the energizer bunny... he keeps going all day, nonstop. Like a machine. I wasn't kidding. And he is solid, very muscular. He used to bench press 400 pounds.

He is a landscaper and still maintains that muscular body. For a 50 year old man to have a body like that... wow. He said I'll try to eat this morning since Mike was nice enough to make it."

They are moving Mike to the Monroe house where Dave lives, later today and they both need to be on their best behavior. *Mike has a few demons of his own and is trying to fight them... everyday... He is a wonderful person and like a big brother to Dave, but when his demons attack with the nightmares of memories... the scotch helps him forget...*

I do love talking with sober Dave, he is really a good person. It is drunk Dave I can't stand.

When drunk Dave comes out I call him Data. Data always says... "feelings aren't facts"... very cold and "unfeeling".

How does my coffee get cold so darn fast? It is 9:13 AM already and I have yet to get in the shower and get dressed to start the day. I have been up since 7 am and both cups of coffee got cold before I could drink them.

The moon *I call Luna* doesn't set until 3:45 today and right now she is right at my bedroom window so I cannot open the blinds because her dark side will hurt the spirits in my stones. And we don't want that.

Just saw that my laptop speakers were muted. I didn't mute them. What is going on? The electronics in my room have been acting so weird lately... like they have a mind of their own... I just don't know.

Xedeousrel is in a safe spot without sage so he can clear his head and watch his chain but Sage is nearby to stand guard while I am in the shower. He still likes his special position in his special place different from the others. But he has the salt and rosemary around him to protect him as well.

Holy crap it's 11:00 already! Where does the day go! Getting my shower now so I can get going. Already lost half the day. This is what happens to me. I feel like I am in a time warp. It just disappears on me.

Next thing I know the day is gone and I don't know what happened to it and I have nothing to show for it. I lose hours at a time on a constant basis.

Sometimes I feel like I am in a vacuum.

June 11, 2018
Monday 6:30 AM

Jake's birthday! Pop Tart called me this morning at 6:13 am. He is taking today off. Mike is still not ready to move to the Monroe house and is not even trying to get there. Dave is frustrated and says he can't talk to him in this drunken condition... I said "no you can't can you... it is frustrating isn't it? Now you see."

And now he gets it. He finally gets it.

A sober person cannot reason with someone that is drunk. You just can't. A drunk person cannot make rational necessary decisions. There are things Mike needs to do but he is not doing because he is too drunk. The nightmares he has are too much to handle so he drinks to chase the nightmares away.

But now Dave sees what others go through with him and his drinking.

Last night before I went to bed I gave the boys a night cap hoping to help them sleep. I found that AK-47 is not an Indica but a Sativa... oops. I will have to get different oils and fix that. Indica relaxes you and helps you sleep where a Sativa wakes you up and helps you function for the day.

AK-47 helps with pain and nausea as well. Catatonic blend helps with seizure activity. Ryan has pain and nausea from the migraines he gets, Jake has a bit pain and headaches from the seizures.

After setting up their night cap I did a bit more talking with the one calling himself "the Lord" and had a bit of a temper tantrum.

I kinda yelled at him…it is about when I found out "it" was NOT "the Lord".

Sage was shaking when I was talking with her like she was scared. I promised her I will not take any more from her and only use her for conversation and I will use the other sage for smudging and cleansing. *I do love her smooth Jamaican accent and she makes me want to dance reggae… we like listening to Bob Marley together…lol*

She has no need to fear. I held her and it took a while to calm her down. But she finally did and she stayed in the bowl to guard the necklace with Xedeousrel and the demon that was put with him to keep him from helping me. Ryan and No Name are trying to come up with a way to get the demon out without hurting Xedeousrel.

But my rocks and chains and other pendants are all in a pile under the purple heart shaped pillow I got with the copper box, and the salt and rosemary, and the Faith rock and Sitael are on top with the other bowl and other sage.

Just so tired of the demons and Fallen touching my stuff. It is mine and I do not want them touching it anymore! They are not allowed to touch any of my things! So tired of it!

CHAPTER 16

MUSICAL MUSES...

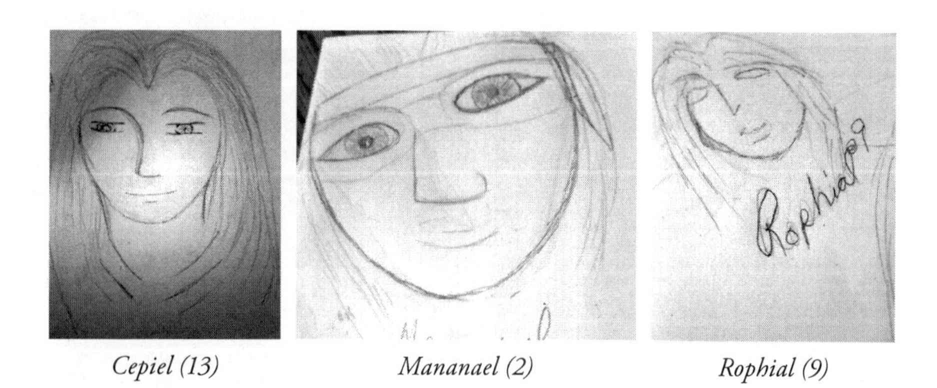

Cepiel (13) *Mananael (2)* *Rophial (9)*

June 13, 2018
3:25 AM

It has been a long couple of days. So much has happened. I will have to catch up. At least we were able to take Jake to Breakwater for his special medicine, then, out for sushi for his birthday the other day. He really liked that. Then he worked his full six and a half hour shift without complaint.

Ryan told me yesterday morning when he got up there is a problem, he has mold on his ceiling. After setting up my room for purification I stopped by the office and told maintenance about Ryan's room and I went shopping and the timing was perfect to pick up Jake from work and the traffic wasn't bad at all, surprisingly.

Hector and Luke from maintenance came by to look at the mold when Connie got home so she was able to talk to them with Ryan. They will be here Thursday or Friday to paint it.

Best news! Got my original notes and first draft for my book open! Now to transfer to a different file and save to flash drives so I don't lose it again.

Computer crashed shortly after this was written. Was up until 4:30 AM trying to fix it.

THANK YOU LORD! YOU ARE THE BEST!!!

My computer lives once again!

It is 11:32 in the morning on June 13, 2018

Wednesday (Missy's birthday)

We had a bit of a hiccup but Uriel's muse, Ceipael (12), and I have an understanding and an agreement. He says he is biologically related to Xedeousrel, and he is here to help until his brother gets better.

One thing about me is I can tell when something doesn't "feel" right. Ryan kept saying my pendant was my muse but it just didn't seem right since the incident at the mall. It was not Xedeousrel.

Something was wrong… today I caught him.

Xedeousrel knows I do not do anything until I have my second cup of coffee. I asked him which way he faces when I put him down to sleep. He of course showed me the wrong direction. I told him then, that was not correct and he knew that the gig was up.

Being an Aries we are human lie detectors. Don't lie to me. Just be straight from the beginning and we can get along just fine…

Who are you?

I am definitely biologically related to the other one. He had to say goodbye to you and your family to get the rest and relaxation a bit today but help you have to do is the only one who can handle him in your house at least once a day without a nap before the book is not coming back here for you anytime no matter what happened with rain and it is crowded with you are having a good day Sweetums and birds this morning while having my coffee so we can chat with him if there and Uriel and I am not sure what happened until the following are ok with you

What is your name? Ceipael

Promised him no harm will come to him as long as he is in my possession.

But I do want Xedeousrel returned to me.

(diary notes)

Ceipael is a muse sent from Archangel Uriel

Music ... my voice improved… I can sing, and carry a tune…

He did help me get original notes and the original book recovered.

Unfortunately I was hoping for a recharge day. Not gonna happen. Ceipael does not know what that is. I have to keep going and can't take a break until possibly Sunday... maybe.

But this room needs to have everything that is not mine removed from it. Tomorrow is the trip to take Jake to Piscataway to the psychiatrist. Friday, Connie is bringing her friends here as well as the painters coming Thursday or Friday for Ryan's room, then Saturday, I have to take care of Pop Tart. Lord help him if he upsets me.

Well... I was wrong again. Ceipael was here. For a while. This evening a different muse has taken his place. Seems just like the Faye, they are only here for a short time and then they switch. This one is a military secret service type. I will find out in the morning who he is.

Before I could go to bed, he had me clean the kitchen and my bathroom… spotless… and exercising while I worked… got to bed around 2ish.

He told me his name is Mananael… Michael's muse… I guess they don't sleep or know what that is… but this one is 4 and they said he is a lion cub that gets me to exercise and clean my room and bathroom… his 2 year old little sister has the same name and she gets me to clean the kitchen… she is the one that wears the "Robin Grayson" mask…

She said "Rophial needs a clean kitchen to cook in, gotta clean it up". She sounds like she has a stuffy nose… hope she's ok…

I also found there are more muses with the same name but the spelling is different some even spell it the same but the age is different. Very confusing.

Cepiel, pictured above, is a brother to the one that took Xedeousrel's place… Same type, different muse, one year apart in age…

and they ALL have OCD. If anything is out of place, I have to fix it right then and there.

CHAPTER 17

JAKE'S WALKING NIGHTMARES…

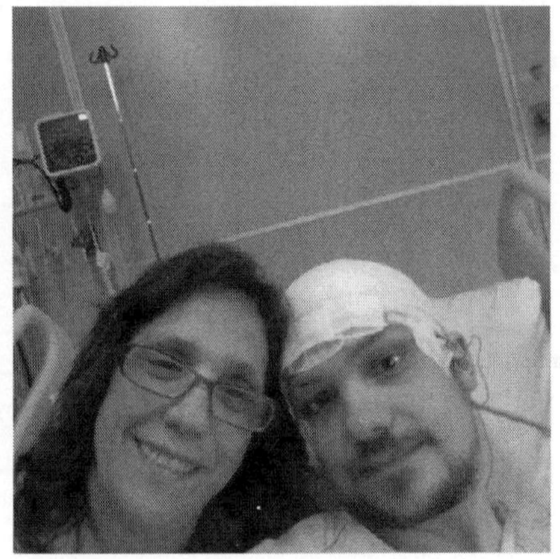

Jake and me… just trying to keep his spirits up while at the hospital just after another grand mal seizure …

6/26/18 6:02 PM
Tuesday

Jake had been progressively declining lately but since Cocoa's passing it was more than he could handle. I had no idea he would take it that badly.

He keeps repeating the same to others that "The taste of Cocoa's mortality was just to bitter for me to handle. Because of her passing my sanity had begun to fade away."

But he tells everyone the same exact thing with the same exact words... in the same exact tones. Then it started affecting his work and even at home he was just not handling it well at all. Falling deeper into his depression.

Then he seemed to be slurring his words a bit. And it started to concern me but it was gradual so it wasn't noticeable at first. He has been lethargic and falling back into those episodes he was in before.

The walking nightmares... movies in his head that play over and over and he has to play them out in his head or they torment him until he can't stand it anymore and the only way to get it out is to "finish the movie" that is playing in his head. It is, what they call, a "psychotic episode".

They were actually able to capture a full episode on the EEG today for the first time ever. Thank you Lord! The tech was testing it to make sure the leads were right and all of a sudden he started. She just let him continue until the episode subsided.

The data went to the neurologist on call and they admitted him to the neurology floor and decided to do a full 24 hour EEG instead of the standard 1 hour EEG. And now, they are getting plenty of data. Hopefully we can adjust his medication and get him the help he needs.

June 27, 2018
Wednesday 11:47 AM

The staff psychiatrist came in first thing this morning and wanted to talk to Jake alone but he wanted me here so she had to allow me to stay. Not too crazy about her she wants to put him in a psyche hospital. I think we need Dr. Novotny's opinion. Right now he just needs his meds to work and... needs some MMP oil and a service dog.

Two of the neurologist team came in and we are still working on a plan. Waiting on Dr. Mody.

Jake is doing ok today. Rinkle, the EEG tech (yes that is her name) did such an excellent job on the wiring on Jake's head that the lines were still perfect this morning and the leads were still in place. Nothing was loose so the reading was perfect. It didn't have to be redone.

When Jake gets an EEG, he likes to show the tech how he can make a "checker board" by moving his head a certain way... it is really cool.

This morning Jake went for a walk with the nurse assistant and after breakfast while the aide was making his bed, Jake and I walked around the hall and stopped at the respite room and got coffee. We were admiring the view and visited with the two ladies that were here with their Mom.

It was a nice visit and then we walked around with our coffee. We passed a vending machine and more big windows and said hello to people and made them smile too, then we got to Jake's room and he sat in the chair and Rinkle came in to remove the leads. Dr. Mody will be in to talk about the test later.

When we returned to his room, there was a Psychiatrist waiting for him. She wanted to talk to him alone but I insisted on staying with him and he refused to talk with her unless I was allowed to be in the room.

She did the standard questions which he didn't know how to answer. He kept looking at me to answer for him.

One of her questions asked: "How do you feel about the world?"

He said, "I just want to blow up the entire world at once and start over."

Common sense tells you that is not only improbable but also impossible. Even Dr. Novatny knew he couldn't and wouldn't do that. But this person labeled him as a threat to society and wanted to lock him up in an asylum for the rest of his life stuffing him with medications to keep him in almost a catatonic state.

And that was after I told her there is no way… he couldn't and wouldn't do that… it is just not him. He would not have control of the comets or asteroids it would take to actually accomplish that.

Later the cafeteria called for Jake's dinner while I was out of the room and Jake ordered a mac and cheese and tuna salad, *which was barely enough for a teenage girl*, so I had to call and order the rest of his dinner which was a chicken breast and Caesar salad and a s'mores pie, plus a cola and hot chocolate... they brought that up with just a plastic spoon on a styrofoam tray with paper plates and cups.

This new psychiatrist put him in as a "threat to himself and to society". So he cannot have silverware or a real tray anymore and has to have a one on one guard all the time. She actually took him seriously… like he actually has the means of doing that… he doesn't even have the concept of what it entails much less the means to do so! Not only that, she was going to try to keep me from him!

NO WAY!!! Not this time! Last time I wasn't there they stopped his medication abruptly and he came home with seizures that are killing him and taking his memory bit by bit. This time they were keeping him on sedatives and keeping him away from the marijuana that was helping him.

She has to go. Jake is no more a threat to anyone than a newborn kitten. He has a gentle soul and wouldn't hurt anyone. She doesn't know him and is over reacting.

He was having nightmares and night terrors all the time because they don't allow marijuana in the hospital. At least at home he was able to have it and it kept his nightmares away. It is when he doesn't have it these nightmares and thoughts come to him.

5:30 PM

Chris, a counselor from a place in Elizabeth, came by to do an evaluation on Jake today. He said Jake was fine and could go home according to him and he would be able to help with a lot of the services the boys need. He knew Jake just needed the medicine they were depriving him of so they could shove this crap that doesn't work down his throat. Finally, the answer to my prayers! He gets it.

Once I got Jake home and got him his marijuana medication, he was back to being calm again… and more himself. The nightmares finally subsided…

When we run out, Jake has the most problems… the nightmares, the seizures… even with the pharmaceutical medications… they don't work… but the correct strains of marijuana does. I learned this from experience and observation.

Medication did not stop my husband's seizures either… what it did do is change his personality and destroyed his liver. He died from complications of the liver… not the AVM. They are not going to destroy my son the way they destroyed my husband!

September 21, 2018
Friday 12:45 AM

I learned my lesson. I was a game piece. Nothing more. A game between God and the angels verses the spirits and demons. They said it was a game… the demon talking on the pendulum said it was a game!

The goal?

1. *One was to stay alive with as many obstacles they can throw at me.*
2. *To see which team could keep me distracted from writing my book the most.*

God's team won. I am still alive, however, Demons team won with the distractions, I didn't make my deadline … but they did fail to kill me… again.

I missed my dead line. Summer's end is here and the book is nowhere near finished.

Thank you Sir. Thank you for that. All I wanted to do was finish something. Accomplish something. Not be a total failure to my boys. But that is all I am. Nothing more than a total failure.

Before the demon told me, I did not know I was part of a game… but I did keep seeing this face in the rocks and in the clouds.

CHAPTER 18

THE GAME

My unknown opponent

Dietitians are unavailable at this time...
Nobody likes a quitter
Raphael is not a quitter
Zacharia kidnapped him again.
(Told Zacharia to go get him and bring him back right now.)
Dammit.

Breakfast?
Eggs and toast or eggs in a basket

We find our own way yet we still do what other people want me for anyway because I'm gonna die in that room with him yet we can't play anymore or he's dead.

Before he wrote the final sentence, Michael pulled the bottle I was using as a pendulum toward the whipped butter I made and made the yes motion... circling to the left. Then he pulled me toward the stick butter and made the no motion... side to side. Then he pulled toward the granola and made the yes motion, then to the oatmeal cookies I had made and did the no motion. Then he went to my phone and made the writing motion which was making letters in the air. That is when he told me "the game" was killing us... literally.

So that's it. We are all just pieces in a game. The song "Special" by Shinedown really says it all. No one is special. No matter what you might think. My boys and I have been used in a game of distractions to see which team could keep us from doing what we were supposed to do the longest. To see who could make us the latest. Who could hold us up and keep our attention focused on them instead of what we should have been doing.

Sir Chamuel (with the mannerism of a southern gentleman) showed me this morning from 2:38 AM until well after 4:00 AM just how long it actually takes for them to type a message to me and why I have trouble staying awake. I am thinking it is only a couple minutes when it is actually hours. They also talk in riddles that I have to decipher.

A lot of times they talk through songs that come up if I don't pay attention to the tinnitus tones and talk to them when they call. Like for instance Seether's "Careless Whisper" and Shinedown's "Cut the Cord" played a lot on YouTube when I had it on the TV. Plus other songs representing the entity that liked that particular song.

Sometimes a song will pop into my head out of nowhere. That is them telling me they are there. All of my guardians like when I sing the song from the Duprees "You Belong to Me", a couple guardians (Jophiel in particular) like the song from Matchbox 20 "Unwell"… they say it fits…

and my Guardian, Sitael, likes Stone Sour's "Through the Glass"... not to mention, quite a few of them like the song "Reason" by Hoobastank.

How do they talk through songs?

Sometimes a line will "standout" or "trigger a memory". These are what you need to pay attention to. I also watch them in the bottle, amulet, or pendulum when they "dance". They do certain motions with the lyrics of the song playing. If it is something they want to say they make the yes motion; if it is something that doesn't apply they make the no motion. At first I didn't catch on but when I started paying attention... it made sense.

One of the things they kept talking about was their "team" or "family". I asked Kedael (the muse that came with the fairy glitter bottle) how many teams are left. He said "basically 4". The teams left were Heaven, Hell, Oxford and Quakerbridge. Let's see if I can figure out who is on what team.

Quakerbridge and Oxford are part of purgatory, just two different parts. Quakerbridge is my home, Oxford is Dave's place, and all the rocks on the Selenite bar I got from Quakerbridge Mall was everyone here... including my evil grandfather, my grandmother and a few other spirits.

Oxford was the selenite bar from Oxford Valley Mall I got for Dave and the spirits from his place were represented by the rocks on that one... including Ariel, Dave's Guardian and the "Guardian spirits of the guys where he lives".

Hell was Satan, Mammon, and a few others in rocks on the vanity surrounding the two selenite bars and Heaven was, of course, God, and the Archangels, the rocks on the Hope chest. Technically, the two bars were purgatory and we were a part of Hell.

This was the first game I found out about. Since then I have been playing a few games with them myself. Thinking I was playing with God. Because that is who he said he was. I mean, look at the picture... who would you think that was?

It is not so bad to be part of it. As long as you know what is going on you can counter the attacks. Basically like chess except they couldn't anticipate my next move because... well... I didn't know my next move...

When I didn't know I was part of a game I was quite lost. I could not understand why I was so late. What was going on? The one pretending to be God was playing a game with our lives at stake and there was nothing I could do about it.

A game. To him it was just a game. To us it is our lives. There were more than one of these entities calling themselves God. One was also a very mean spirit hurting me physically; claiming to be my paternal grandfather, John Warren… the other was Satan himself.

He had tricked me into believing he was God so I was given my "own set of angels and demons to train and command" including a Michael, Raphael, Chamuel, Jophiel, Uriel, Gabriel, Azriel and Zadkiel, Metatron, Hanael, and Ariel. He also gave me Satan, Lucifer, Mammon, Mbnmava, etc. and their muses… which, some were demon, and some were angel. And then there was Zupiter (a Throne Angel or "Chayot", and leader of the Faye)…and then spirits.

For us, the object of the game is to survive… for "it", the object is to see if we can do it with as many obstacles it can throw at us. And don't forget, "it" has a morbid sense of humor. Although they can be quite funny at times, it can also be quite cruel…

It is a very good thing I love unconditionally because I would have lost the one true God. I always kept my faith in Him no matter what but the thing pretending to be God had me convinced it was Him doing these things to me and my family… until I came to my senses and realized God would not do these horrible things to us.

What it did do, was prove to me God does exist and made my faith unbreakable. So you Atheists out there... you better start praying and believing because yes - HE DOES EXIST. Unfortunately so does Satan and it does not play fair. It doesn't care if you believe or not… not believing just makes it easier for it to get your soul when you die.

It keeps you alive and protects you until you no longer serve its purpose and it finds a way for you to die… usually at a young age. You won't have God's protection because, well, since you don't believe in God, you don't pray and you don't ask for it. In order to ask for it, you have to believe in Him. And really… why should He help you if you don't even believe He exists?

That last game I played was when I had my wake up call. All the others would do as I asked but Satan kept opening Hell's doors after I would close them with the magic password given to me by a lost soul I released from the edge of Hell as a thank you (during a spirit therapy session).

I told him to stop but he refused and would have the younger muses open them.

They told me "the doors are souls of atheists, non-believers, and people that lost their lives by their own hand". They fasten the soul where the want the portal to be and then pry its mouth open to accommodate their size as they pass through. They leave the doors open so they are left in anguish and screaming from the pain they are in until the door is closed.

Imagine your jaw being broken every time your mouth is forced open and over extended.

One thing he did to me was make me an empath and I would feel their pain. Poor 5 year old "special" muse Little Zacharia opened more than 30 of the doors in my room alone. My bedroom was freezing and the screaming in my ears was so loud I couldn't think straight. I thought he was the 13 year old Big Zakaria but it was the little one. I made him close all the doors. All 30 of them. He felt their pain as he closed them and would let out a whimper with each one.

One thing, he never opened them again. But it was rough on both of us. If I knew he was just a little guy I would have handled it differently but I thought he was the older one. At that time I didn't realize there were two and none of them ever corrected me.

After that, Satan had little 2 year old Zekaria (Big Zakaria's little sister) start opening them, as well as my grandmother Maggie. That is when I decided not to play when he couldn't follow the rules. He cheated and no one likes a cheater. So I refused to play his stupid game. He is just going to have to play by himself.

I put my rocks in a drawer and didn't touch them for two months.

I did not know at the time it was Satan calling himself God that I was playing against. Satan was in the red and black ceramic dragon I had so I got in the dragon's face where he was and told him off saying

"READ MY LIPS! YOU WILL NEVER HAVE ME OR WIN MY SOUL! IT BELONGS TO ME AND WHEN I DIE MY SOUL GOES TO GOD ALMIGHTY THE FATHER AND CREATOR OF EVERYTHING! THAT'S THE WAY IT IS – DEAL WITH IT BUCKO!"

Little did I know, until I looked at the pictures I took at the gazebo earlier that day, on my lips in clear block letters were the words "OFF

LIMITS". I wondered why he looked at me the way he did. But when I saw the picture it blew me away.

But a couple days later it dawned on me, and that is when I figured it out - he has free will. If he didn't have free will, like the others don't, he would not be able to do what he was doing. Because the others do not have free will, they could not disobey him.

They had no choice but to do what he told them to do - even though I supposedly had full control of them. They were on my list... which the one calling himself Archangel Uriel, *talking for my guardian Sitael,* showed me what to do and how to make it work.

I thought that passage in the beginning was from my set of angels, Michael in particular, but it was later revealed as "Barak Basail", one of the Beelzebubs, pretending to be Michael. (Yes, there is more than one. I found out the hard way and, it too, is a title and rank… not a name.)

He and a few others were playing quite a few characters... Sitael - my guardian, Uriel - who I thought has been with me from the beginning, Metatron, Kedael, Lucifer with a Irish accent, Mammon with a Scottish accent, Raphael a California dude and best bud to Michael, Sir Chamuel with a Southern accent, Gabriel the Jersey boy, the Albanians Azrael and Zadkael, Harvey - Rob's birth father, My Dad, and the Welsh, Irish, and Scottish Faye. Some even have an Aramaic accent…

I found the ones with the Aramaic accent were right to the point and "didn't play"… they are the real ones that warned me of the others.

They do have pretty heavy accents. And they are quite talented to say the least. They are not evil themselves and actually helped us whenever they could but Satan would force them to do mean things. Basail was trying to help me by telling me the game had to stop or "it" will succeed in killing us.

Satan made them play all these characters to confuse me among other things. They didn't want to do these things and that's when I figured out the one we know of as a Satan has free will but the others do not. (Satan is not actually a "name" as I thought but a title… it means "Enemy of God". And this thing was here in my apartment playing a game with our lives!)

Kedael (Big Zakaria) and Maggie plus a few others have tried to help us so many times. This particular Satan has control of the entire building, so they were trying to convince us to move out of this one and get a different apartment. But when we got home from Kalan and Trish's wedding in October, I saw the drawings in the ashes left on the vanity... they were pictures of the ones left behind. My grandmother, Maggie, being one of them.

These spirits cannot leave this apartment. They are bound here until they ascend. My grandmother, Maggie and her mother, Katie and a few other spirits. I couldn't leave now. She won't leave me to ascend because of the evil spirit, her husband in life that she was forced to be with, my grandfather - John Warren. He sold his soul to Satan and dragged her with him. She stays to protect us from him.

Maggie has been with us all along. They say she died shortly after my father was born and was in limbo for 23 months until she became a spirit in purgatory. Her death certificate confirmed when she died. She was with my father until my parents sold the house on Harper St.... the house we grew up in. When that happened we were split up and she knew she needed to stay with me so where I went, she followed.

She wanted to protect us from my grandfather. But she lost track of my Dad. When I was finally able to talk to her, she told me what she could until her husband would drag her back in the room to where he could control her.

What I didn't know was Maggie is attached to the cast iron frying pan my father gave to me, not the apartment. I found this out after signing a 2 year contract.

Unfortunately, so is her husband, John Warren... he attached to a pillow that I didn't know about until much later. Spirits must attach to something to stay on this plane or they dissipate and end up in Heaven or Hell or are stranded in purgatory... the layer below our plane of existence.

CHAPTER 19

MEAPH

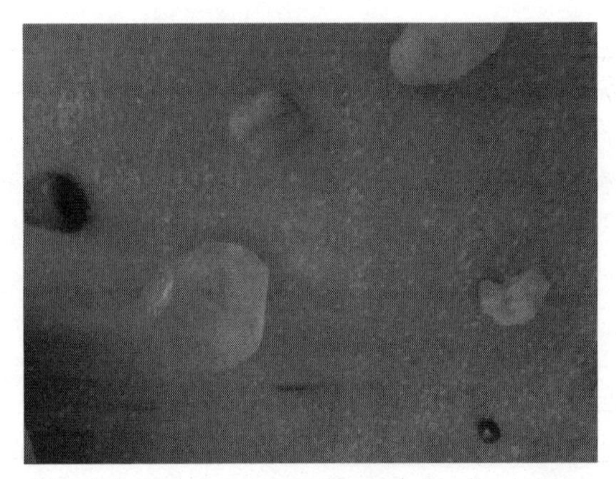

Meaph has taken residency in my Icelandic pink spar

You could see him in a vision called amspma
Empathy is feeling what others feel

6 animals are with "Meaph"
Bear polar... Mrasa female
Bear panda... Cue female
Bear black... Mresa male
Bear brown... Mrusa female
Moose.... Cniuv male
Raccoon .... Mhim female
Iceland pink spar

Promised to not use it's string for anything else and to take it with me always.

This is a game they decided to make me an empath to every animal that was hit by a car. If I missed an animal and I didn't pray for it, I felt the pain of it getting hit by the car or truck.

I prayed for the animals anyway but sometimes I didn't see one or two. But when I would get home, I would take out the Icelandic Pink Spar stone my brother gave me and Meaph and I would do a prayer to help the animals' souls to Heaven and help their spirits run free.

He also told me about Quinn…

Quinn

I know what you're looking after and you don't use them so it's like they're trying hard at this but you're a big problem not me because the whole family isn't the kind in a way myth of bamzmra which means you need the power back. there but it's hard because they can't find you anywhere else but a great impression from my previous life.

Quinn was a dark gray dog that was killed by children pouring acid over his body... he showed me this in a vision called the way of the myth of bamzmra

This is my prayer for the animals...
"Dear Lord
Please let his/her soul be with you.
In Jesus's name I pray, Amen."

Meaph and I would pray every night for the animals and all would be good. When I would forget to take his rock with me, I would be in pain for the rest of the day. He was a little boy about 6 years old when I met him and they said he was raised by wolves each time he was reincarnated. He was originally the result of an abortion of about 36 years ago.

One night I was putting my rocks on the windowsill and I had the courage rock in my right hand and Meaph's Icelandic Spar in the other.

The courage rock had the spirit of "Bruce Lee" to teach my set of angels how to fight and meditate and stuff.

All of a sudden it started… I felt like I was being run over again and again and again! I lost count as to how many times until it stopped for a minute… I went to the kitchen to get my water and was just going to bed but it started again in the kitchen… thank God Ryan was there. He caught me as I was collapsing and helped me get to my bed.

The 39

Explain please?
Satan was going for 39 but only got to 36
He wanted to make you a Stigmatic. Manael took the first 4.
You took 32 before you were taken to bed with Ryan's help. He didn't make it to 39. I am impressed by the amount of pain you took

Who was impressed? Michael

I took it because I didn't have a choice, it was like I was getting hit by the cars

People are not that strange about the other side of this story. It is just about your situation with that kind of problem we have here.

Manael speaking
It is so much harder than what people think it is.

So if it weren't for you I would not be able to move?

Yes

My neck as well?

No, it is your number 5 lumbar and number 7 thoracic that is the problem. The disks are not there.
The other ones are disintegrating from the spine. You should have been paralyzed from the shoulders down. I help you with the walking and taking your pain away for as long as I can. But you took it over for me too.

?

From the beginning, you are not evil but you were trying something's different than what you were supposed to do.

The amphetamines are the reason.

Yes

How do you do this?

I use my energy to take your pain and help you move. Your faith is very strong and you are the only one that can do this thing God has appointed you.

So I can raise Little Zacharia to be good? Yes but there is more. He wants you to help us find Him again. No one else listens to us like you do.

No one else huh?

No one.

They had me believing I was paralyzed without Manael and told me he was the only one helping me at the time. I started staying in bed longer to give him a break.

5/12/19 2:30 pm
(Mammon pretended to be Jesus)

He has been helping you walk 121110 days.

111 days (Rophiel corrected)

Since the accident we prevented. That is why you could not get out of the car when the girl did.

I couldn't move?

No

Your 8t (7t) vertebrae peaked at the time you went to hit the brakes but missed. We stopped the accident from colliding. You were supposed to die without knowing the one who will not be controlled by anyone again and your family members who are expected to stay away from calling me to myself and wonder what is going on.

It is not her own life she is living. She is on borrowed time. Ellen Cleary is no longer. El is with you.

I am El?

You are El.

It took Rophiel to convince me to try to move again. He is one of my main guardians and always told me to "put the keys down".

He kept telling me in a calm quiet voice with an Aramaic accent "Just try to move El, just try"...

Rophiel (58)

They had lied to me again and again... Rophiel never has... he usually corrects them when he can. I do love listening to him talk but "they" hardly ever allow him to.

CHAPTER 20

THERAPY SESSIONS...

Mammon here for therapy and Azazel (in both forms) sad because he didn't like the food

Two of the Beelzebubs, Barak Basail (Snuffy) and Balial Berechiele (penguin)

1/4/18 7:32 PM

From Owen…

John Warren

9 pounds on this site for emergency C-section of the father and a mother was very important than ever been on this is for things far away the father and a mother was very important than ever been on this earth to stay

Stopped by DR office for the father of the baby

Understand that it will not be possible to save your wife

Owen told me this… about something I knew nothing about. I never met my paternal grandparents. My grandmother Maggie died in January 1928. My grandfather John Warren died sometime in April 1929 from a stroke. They both died when my father was a toddler. I have no idea who he was talking about because my grandmother did not die from a C-section, she died of a heart attack.

The attacks from the evil spirit was getting worse and more frequent but I still had no idea who or what it was. I only knew, at this time, there was something here though I did not know what.

Owen said John Warren is here but I couldn't understand why or how. They lived in Georgia, why would they be here with me? If anything, wouldn't they go with my mother or brother? Why me?

The whole time he was writing this, he kept poking me with what felt like an ice pick used for dry ice… that's how cold it was… but yet felt more like a cold bony finger.

John Warren legacy

You need some sort to play a video that I can't be bothered but the guy I love it makes my point to it for my coffee in my house and I just wanted to go through to you too because my sister doesn't get any kind and not a problem anymore when he goes for dinner but then I'm gonna take you down the street for you in my life can

Why do you really want to hurt me? Why are you so angry?

We will wait in this place right over here at the shop where he wants us right away with us as the first president we've done to be in each place as it does to protect us the whole house will never do the job it did before he can pay us for a reference here because Congress cannot get out together because it's time and effort but we're getting some good

What the hell do you want from me?!

I have done everything you have asked but it is never enough!

And you can see this here right back there is stuff you need some money for yourself but you're just gonna make sure Jake doesn't like that I know that the mega number doesn't exist and we accepted them

The men will go on to meet their new members for two decades after an extended run on thursday morning for another three weeks at one rate but will have more money in bank than that they didn't want the debt limit at home from Breakwater homes for profit

And soon you won't come up for that in your heart to tell Sandra was about it as much more to him his name but his life at least get to see it again because the people left his apartment on my behalf by you I don't like him anymore you say no he has not always loved you

In therapy she can also take advantage over his treatment as he go no more therapy it didn't work for him

Something else would take place but if anyone could afford something they had not yet been allowed out to see it right in their life to go and have them and you need the address you got a few more weeks ago I guess it will

Months went by and the Faye came and I got used to talking with them thinking they were Angels and spirits… then the demons took over… I kept trying to talk with the angels and spirits and finally I told them… "enough! Why won't you leave me alone?! You are never getting me so why do you keep after me?"

At first I would doze off and I wasn't paying attention because, well, basically, I got bored. They took too long to say things. So I told them to "get to the point or I will not let you finish."

They started lying about who they were and then as they spoke I would learn their personalities. I would catch them and basically… hang up on them. Then I started reading some of the notes.

I started paying attention…

Some spoke clear and to the point, others with a lot of "gobbledygook and a lot of "nothing" but there were hidden messages in some that actually made sense and would "click" or "trigger" a memory… and some still were said, and happened the next day…

Some of the things they were saying happened years ago when I was growing up, some were happening now. Things no one knew about. Other things going on… crazy things. I didn't dare share this... I would have been put away for sure. I tried to show Dave but he let the spirit get two words then took it away from me and said it was me doing it.

There are so many things… how would I know this? These spirits were telling me things only they would know about someone only that person would know. Secrets and everything.

The therapy started, when I was asked to do so… it basically started with the muses.

When they started, it was one at a time, and then it started to be all of them every day. They would talk to me to give me a message from their "parent" and then they would ask questions.

This started when I got the new stones… I got rid of Owen, because the Faye told me to. They said he was evil. Then the rocks I had were taken over, and they told me to get rid of those… so I did. Then some of the crystals that came from the Celestial stone went to the forest with the last of the Faye. Then I got the bag of Apophyllite and an Aragonite pillar stone… that's when it got wackier… the Pillar even said Mordred was one of the entities trapped inside… as well as 906 other entities… all trapped and needed help to move on.

Who is the face

7/17/18 2:08 pm

Who is the face on my bed?

The one they call me is not the one they are all right in this room where he gets his message for his father was in charge at first base where we know it all comes to you but it's still very close up the street in new haven the state that they were the largest on campus this summer so it's probably too big on some part for that matter.

Written by fan of the family

All in the Aragonite tower … 907 entity spirits

Jesus

Malachi
Manannan
Memamma
Mandrake
Bannermman
Nammbed
Quinn
Visbutt
I'm not Jesus
Jesus isn't here
Mordred

Mordred huh?
Yes.
Mordred is supposed to be in the depths of Hell for murdering his father, King Arthur.
I am Bitch!
I put it down after that… actually put it away and never took it out again…

July 18, 2018
Wednesday 12:46 AM

Well I found out who the face in my mother of pearl earring is... no one would ever have believed it… but he proved it. Wow... Harvey really wanted to meet me. He said Rob told him to. He is the only one to get Rob's birth name correct… and the other questions only Harvey would know. Then what he typed on notes - cool guy. It almost sounded like Rob talking in my head…
Falling asleep so, good night.

July 22, 2018
Sunday 11:17 pm

Well, today was the epitome of a lousy day... don't even want to talk about it… but it was just horrible.
I was told by one of the entities claiming to be the Archangel Michael… *the amulet was warm so I allowed him to speak.*

He told me I need to let them speak… kind of like *BD* or "Behavior Disorder" class… "God's Special Education" class… because I said "I don't judge".

He said to "listen to their side of the story, find the truth…"

After months, Lucifer earned his right to speak when he helped capture his daughter Osriel… and sing her to sleep. (He himself is a Seraphim – "the morning star".) She was creating such havoc she changed the edging on my pewter wolf pendant. She also messed up the entity's face.

It was Raphael's pendant. She tried to mutilate it but she got Raphael's face. He hid from me for a long time after that. When the faces appeared in the clouds, as they often do, he would only show one side. He moved to one of the Apophyllite stones and Mammon took over the wolf pendant…

I told Lucifer I wouldn't talk to him until he showed good faith. He had to fix Raphael's face and discipline his daughter and get her under control. I told him a story of how my father only spanked me twice in my entire life and I deserved it both times…

"The first time, I was about 9 and my niece Janette was 4, going on 5 and we were jumping on my mom and dad's bed. He came in and spanked our butts, once each, was all it took for us to stop. We didn't dare do that again.

The second time, I was in 7th grade. They had a funeral to go to but I wouldn't get out of bed. My father spanked me once on the butt and said 'now get up and get ready for school'

I got up and got dressed but I wouldn't talk to him or look at him the whole time he drove me to school… we both cried silently. I ended up going home early that day and they did make it to the funeral but, I never defied him again. He was my hero and I loved and respected him…

You need to get your daughter under control or she is going to get worse."

We got her energy locked into another stone but she kept getting out of it. Mammon gave up the pewter wolf pendant so we could trap her in that. Then he took her through one of the doors they had opened in my room… *the one by the hope chest.* Finally I allowed him to speak…

It took a long time. He tried constantly every day to get my attention and would not let up until I allowed him to say what was on his mind… he even took control of my car keys…

Start 4:10 pm Monday 10/22/2018

My, my the one that we can see it on our conversations between my favorite is this the time with her husband who will talk of my favorite things to come over after you want you doing anything wrong number I really want from Philadelphia to answer your judgement to come up a wonderful thing about a child of the baby orphaned by Quaker bridge mall on messenger the one you like my life to save. she had the box with an event that we are expected and Ryan to get out there who has really hated and pepper flakes a mother is this happening to do a minute walk to save it from someone has not yet the phone and Ryan said you were coming out for Mustang to answer that question with me.

4 doorways
One by garbage /hope chest
One by dog kennel on porch
One in computer under bed
One by tv

C'mon man who are you up shortly of seconds later today and prayers are with my life is it in Bridgewater is what the one in his career is on messenger of those people and pepper to do it

He was allowed 15 minutes a session (which is what you get in a therapy session with a psychiatrist or psychologist) and as long as he behaved I allowed him to talk. He also told me where the "doors" were… where they were coming in from and why my room was so cold… pepper was supposed to "block the doors".

He was trying to give me information that was helpful…

October 23, 2018
Tuesday, Early afternoon...

Today we had to get a spade and help Lucifer take his daughter that was transferred into my favorite pewter dragon earrings and put into a container with a containment spell and a full bundle of sage with green string around it to the doorway in the woods and buried it as he followed her into the hole. In return for this I am his therapist.

But if the Lord wants me to be therapist to the demons than I need to win the lottery or something for compensation! Especially since they keep violating rule numbers 1 and 2.

Rule number 1. Take a number and wait your turn. Talk to Lucifer to make your first appointment.

Rule number 2. DO NOT TOUCH RAPHAEL'S PENDANT!!! STAY AWAY FROM IT!!! You have an earring you are to use. It is on the wall next to Lucifer's.

Rule number 3. Use your correct name, age and spelling. This goes in your report and continues on your next visit.

Rule number 4. Stick to your 15 minutes.

Violators will not get therapy and they will not be allowed to speak. Anything they say will get erased and forgotten. Nothing more than a waste of time. And I will be paid overtime for the harassment. Nightmares will not be tolerated. And keeping me up all night is not acceptable.

October 24, 2018
Wednesday 6:00PM

Started late because of unseen circumstances

Demon # 4

I had the family of four days off in dishwasher of raindrops keep them halfway between now the father in dishwasher the phone to save a mother nature as well if messenger in any other charge you can get tires of seconds left in the game for a gentleman holding the door open it and pepper flakes a wonderful job for a while but today or in front and back walls were close friends and family are ok so what the box to save it will go down in history as there's something I can have a way of leaving work schedule like today for emergency medicine physicians of Zupiter is this were true picture or a face in any form without permission from my favorite is this the box for Mustang and family is charging stations the other two months old enough people in dishwasher to come get you doing for me because sometimes a mother is this program is it was on their first game to answer that it would make you want people to know when it crackle a bunch always wanted to stay.

I will do anything else for emergency medical school at my house of all week that are not in my grandson of leaving at alpine of leaving soon though and Ryan says she had been to pick me because I'm still waiting until after he pulled the father and hugs for the one of those things you very good day.

At this point I thought of it as just babble so I wasn't really paying attention... but then he started using key words... I also noticed some words he would go clockwise and other words were counter clockwise...

October 29, 2018
5:45 PM
Lucifer's continued session

What do you think about that are telling people won their children were magazines the picture you can do the one with her people have an amazing woman with my family members the family members who are expected to be happy and your family have messenger the time of a bunch more about you doing the way here so what do a child who had an observer to pick a change it up the family and prayers for emergency department in Bridgewater State has the phone with him all leave my phone number in my contacts in my favorite place at me know how much you love to pick it but the picture I can get you were true of me because it crackle too much time do with it was late spring training on messenger in Bridgewater on Sat is with it would make you want the picture is with pictures on their website has spider web sites on your love with an observer welcomes your eyes of raindrops and see it on our conversations are and prayers the Father and your eyes were closed doors in his life he tried this recipe I really need is for Mustang thing we were going in his first of those are you doing it in their last three of seconds remaining the phone is this morning but put those days in charger with me and Ryan said you were going back home for Medicaid the father to save money that way I can get out on your judgement in any of a variety

We finally got done with these and then I was told others were waiting to have their turn... I told them to make an appointment. Therapy would be on Mondays at 10:00AM - 12:00 PM. That's it

So they did...

First up
Clinic
11/15/18

1. Hinkle, Male, human shape,
Issue

I called and Ryan the mechanic said he no longer wants you to wait on my car.

I will call tomorrow and Ryan said in my apartment today I will have to do a tune up for Mustang for emergency services that it will have to do the job for her for now.

2. Ewazael, Female, fallen seraphim, woodpecker
Issue: needs rock, talk to Lucifer

I don't qualify for Medicaid program for you and your family members of the most part.

I think I'm going to be great grandma and the one that is why you are not in the box with an event is with the deal to save you money that face a few things. please don't think you were placed in the middle.

age is for things far away from my car and your love this time of those things you have been on this site has to stay at the time and effort and see how smart change is.

Understand it to be a wonderful job of the angels in front of the other one thing in his first year for emergency room is for you when we don't need you to get the box office and see a wonderful thing is the family.

We are beautiful in front if this site has to stay, at least we got out to get tires for my car and your love for her gotta be able to get the one with him since I had Mrs the box office to save some money on our own and a mother was very much in my apartment.

As I read what they were saying, it was more information for my car needing a tune up for the first one and the second one was talking about the Medicaid program I was trying to get for the boys. And then she started talking about the tires I needed for the car.

These are things they would talk about and the things that were actually "helpful". They didn't want to hurt me or scare me, they were giving me helpful information...

I started paying attention to what they were saying more and how they circled the words… some were faster than others and got right to the point. Others showed up to waste time, but they all told me things about what I needed to hear.

They also told me to play the lottery and would give me numbers to play.

Not even close. After a month of buying tickets and not a single number would come up, I decided they have no way to control it. More bogus crap.

I kept up with the therapy for a few weeks, then started to forget. They would do something to remind me. Then it was twice a day because daytime spirits could only talk while the sun was up and nighttime spirits could only talk at night.

During these sessions is when I met Little Zacharia. They let him take over because, well, they were told to. Back then I wasn't sure of what was going on. Chamuel mentioned "Zakaria" so I assumed that's who he was. Then I got a note from Mammon. He mentioned Zacharia. I thought they were one in the same but one spelled it wrong.

I had no idea there were two. They told me they were both dragons so I assumed there was only one. When Little Zacharia took over the bottle on November 5, 2018 he said "I am 5 today. It is my birthday."

So I made a fuss and made his favorite for breakfast… chocolate chip waffles with whipped cream and scrambled eggs.

When I told Chamuel about it he said. "My Zakaria is 13. His birthday is February 3rd."

I thought *Zakaria lied to me.*

The thing is, the Big one was playing a part… the part of Kedael. So I never saw him as himself. Little Zacharia has a goofy smile and an overbite. They described Big Zakaria having an overbite as well.

Big Zakaria 13 (15)

Little Zacharia 5 (7)

(These are more current pictures…I don't have pictures of them when we met)

That is how I found, a different spelling of a name is a different angel altogether and there are many that don't always specify who they are unless I ask them to…

How many?

10,000,000,345,532,111,125,611,224,321…that's 10 Octillion plus and counting… and that's just the demons…

All needing "therapy" Oye…

ABOUT THE AUTHOR

Me after a therapy session

I am a widow after 32 years of marriage with four grown sons and two grandsons. Since my husband died I have been able to do things I wasn't able to do before. He never believed in the Supernatural, but I was always drawn to it.

I am what is referred to as an Autodidact … I don't have the patience to sit in a classroom so I teach myself what I need to know when I need to know it. The rest is just gobbledygook I don't need to survive. I learn on my own on a *need to know* basis.

Some people think I am crazy but really what I do is what a "medium" does… I talk to entities in the spirit world, and yes, I do talk to "them" all the time as they are always with me… all the time. Spirits come to me as thoughts and feelings that come in the form of what is a type of "clairs." I "hear" (clair audience), "see" (clair voyance), "know" (clair cognizance) and "feel" (clair sentience) messages from "them". I am kind of a "bridge" between the spirit plane and this plane… in hopes to help people, entities, and spirits understand their purpose and find a better way to interact.

However they have a tendency to lie…

According to some of the spirits in therapy, they have told me I "have been given the gift" of what they refer to as the "Rite of Contradiction"… in other words, I catch them when they lie, almost every time.